About
SNAPSHOTS
Of Our Lives

A stirring collection of anecdotes by three writers looking back over the years, recording their experiences in their native land and as immigrants abroad. These stories cover times of conflict and stability, growing up and in maturity, in sometimes humorous, but always in an honest manner that readers will relate to with a yearning and nostalgia to which every expat can relate.

—Ken Puddicombe: Editor—
MiddleRoad Publishers
www.middleroadpublishers.ca

ALSO BY THE AUTHORS

RAM JAGESSAR
The Man Who Broke The Lottery

ROOP MISIR
OAC Biology Workbook (Student's Manual)
OAC Biology Workbook (Teacher's Guide)

KEN RAMPHAL
Slippery Ochro
(*3rd Prize Guyana Prize For Literature: Fiction 2023*)

Seeram's Illusions
Escape to the Canadian Jungle
Dilchand Joins the Army
Teacher Ram's Fascination With Fire

SNAPSHOTS
Of Our Lives

Ram Jagessar
Roop Misir
Kennard Ramphal

MiddleRoad | Publishers

www.middleroadpublishers.ca

"Making Literature see the light of day."

Library and Archives Canada Cataloguing in Publication

ISBN 978-1-990765-31-5 (paperback)

Cover photos
Guyana: Kaieteur Falls and Legislature by Ken Puddicombe
Trinidad: Hanuman Statue by Ken Puddicombe
Port Of Spain by Anthony Mendenhall
Canadian map: pexels-anna-nekrashevich-7144745
Regions of Guyana: pexels
Trinidad And Tobago: pexels

Layout: Ken Puddicombe
Front Cover Design by Kathryn Lagerquist
Kathryn.lagerquist@gmail.com

What I see is the millions of people, of whom I am just one,
made orphans: no motherland, no fatherland, no gods, no mounds
of earth for holy ground, no excess of love which might lead to the
things that an excess of love sometimes brings, and worst and most
painful of all, no tongue...
—Jamaica Kincaid—

DEDICATION

ROOP MISIR
To my wife Ramdai, son Anil, and daughters Renuka and Nina,
and all those who inspire me.

KEN RAMPHAL
To the people who touched my life with their laughter, kindness
and tears. All of who are responsible for who I am.

ACKNOWLEDGMENTS

KENNARD RAMPHAL

The author wishes to thank all the people who touched his lives when their paths intersected. Most of the people described in the book have "gone to the other shore," but will always be loved. Thanks for all the love, laughter, and lessons you taught me.

ROOP MISIR

To all those who encouraged me to put together my collection of Snapshots, I say: *Thank you.*

Literature is regarded as the mirror of life. I was fortunate to live in two countries, first in British Guiana (Guyana) and later in Canada. To me, writing my snapshots was a trip back in time. It is my fervent hope that readers experience the thrill of being teleported between locations without crossing the intervening space of distance and time.

Table of Contents

BOOK ONE

~THE HOMELAND~

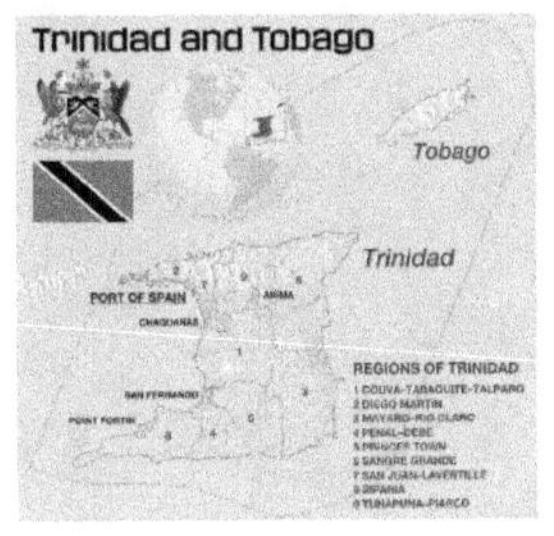

1 CANE FARMING IS SHARP by Ram Jagessar

My first job in the Trinidad Express in 1974 was as an agriculture reporter, which gave me a chance to jump on my trusty Honda 350 monster motorcycle and wheel out to all parts of the countryside for stories.

One of the most inflamed controversies was the issue of cane farmers getting a fair price for their sugarcane from the major buyer, Caroni Limited. Another issue was for the new Cane Farmers' Union getting its members away from the stooge union that helped fix their prices at a low level.

The Cane Farmers' Union called a strike and some of its members stopped selling cane to Caroni Ltd. However, some of the bigger cane farmers who supported the stooge union did not support the strike and sold cane to Caroni.

War was declared in the sugar belt. Some unknown folks began burning young cane fields, destroying its value. It was war in the media too, and the *Trinidad Guardian* supported Caroni and the stooge union through its reporter Mikey Mahabir. He was not exactly popular in rebel cane farmers' circles.

The *Trinidad Express* relied on my coverage and naturally being a rebel myself, I covered the sugar war with much more favourable reports from the strikers' point of view. I could visit the war zone anytime, or so I thought.

One day I thought I would visit one of the cane farmers strike camps, and get some first-hand comments from striking farmers and their union. I pulled into the camp one bright, sunny morning, took off my crash helmet, pulled out my reporter's notebook and confidently strode up to a group of strikers.

Instantly one man in the group grabbed me by the front of my shirt, and put a long shining cutlass at my neck. I froze—trembled, actually. I can't remember. I saw *Yamraj* the god of death, and for a very long moment time stood still. All I could see was the blade at my neck and the stubble of the man's beard so close to me.

Then what felt like an eternity later, I heard the man say to his friends that this was the nasty reporter from the Guardian and he was going to deal with me. It felt like a very long time later that one of his buddies shouted that I was the man from the Express, not the hated Mikey Mahabir, and he should ease up on the cutlass. The man with the blade reluctantly released my shirt and removed his stubble and shining cutlass from my glazed eyesight.

My shoulders slumped, I think my reporter's notebook fell to the ground and I relaxed my clenched sphincter. How I didn't pee myself I have no idea.

With trembling legs, I hurriedly collected some comments, donned my helmet and sped away from that place, hoping never to return.

Let them fight their war among themselves, I thought, as my trusty motorcycle increased the miles between us.

2 SWIMMING BRIDGE DAYS by Roop Misir

My hometown of Windsor Forest was a rice-farming community in Guyana. It was well-known for a ghat—a step or a flight of steps on the south side of the road leading to the water's edge outwards, a place where people would meet, greet, and take a dip. They could mingle with returning fellow field workers heading home after the day's work. Some would take baths or simply wash their hands, feet, and faces. Others simply chatted and gossiped about the latest happenings. The ghat was nicknamed, Swimming Bridge.

As for me, I blended in nicely with people at the ghat at the edge of the Middlewalk Dam. The ghat marks the end of a 5-mile-long irrigation trench bringing fresh creek-water from the water conservancy in the back lands of Boeraserie Creek. Always slow but free flowing, its herbal aroma gives the black water a magnetic pull for people near and far.

Every school day after teaching, I dropped off my school materials at home, picked up my swimming trunks, and bicycled to Swimming Bridge. After *Curtsies* and *Hellos*, I would do my usual routine—jump into the creek and start my swimming session, freestyle. Usually, I would swim half of this canal upstream, then return to the ghat, a combined distance of approximately 5 miles.

CHALLENGES AHEAD

The irrigation canal served as the main transportation route to and from the rice fields and the hinterlands. People commuted in canoes, and flat-bottomed boats using paddles; some even in Evinrude-powered speed boats. And as if the busy traffic wasn't enough, there was the rich diversity of life forms—flora (sedges, water hyacinth, elodea), and fauna (fish, e.g., tilapia), and reptiles (e.g.: snakes and alligators). Water traffic was usually busy, made much more challenging when speed boats raced along Middlewalk, making waves and disturbing the aquatic inhabitants—that would jump into the air like trained dolphins dancing for onlookers at a Canadian Water Park!

Despite these apparent distractions, I felt that it was okay for me to swim as long as I was prepared to share the waterway with all and sundry.

One day, the middle traffic was heavy. A speeding boat came very close to crashing into me. Involuntarily, I swam into what looked like an alligator's nest. To protect her brood, Mother Gator chased me off. Miraculously, I managed to reach safety on the Middlewalk Road.

One on-looking passerby asked, "Aren't you scared now?"

"Yes, I am. I know I should swim when traffic is slow," I replied.

Since then, villagers often reminded me that swimming was risky and I should find a more serene, secure bathing place by the nearby train line than Swimming Bridge. However, neither people nor animals bothered me in the least. It was as if they all recognized my presence, as a kind of ecological harmony, a *deja vu* of sorts. To me, the risks were minimal, and mine to take. And fellow citizens appeared pleased to see me in action, swimming in harmony with the natural world.

Two weeks later, my friend, Jaisingh, was driving the family's new Massey Ferguson tractor on the Middlewalk Road, with a number of his friends perched on top, standing room only. They were celebrating, merrily clapping their hands and singing the Hindi song from the movie, *Deedar. O Bachpan ke din bhula na dena*, which translated into English is, *Oh, don't forget the days of childhood.*

In an apparent attempt to impress me while swimming, Jaisingh let go of the steering wheel and joined the others clapping and sit-dancing. Suddenly, the wheels of the tractor hit a mud bump, the driver lost control and the tractor landed in the trench, barely missing me.

I was scared to death, and nearly pooped my pants! Instantly, the revelers abandoned the tractor, fled the scene, and left me to fend for myself. As for the tractor in the trench, Jaising's father hired a man with a dragline to salvage the submerged tractor and I never saw him driving the tractor from that day on.

Thankfully, passersby dove into the trench and rescued me.

As we say in Guyana: *You can't blow a whistle and suck sugar cane at the same time.*

That was a close call with danger. I got away by the skin of my teeth!

The following week, I left for Canada.

3 RAMADHIN'S ROOSTER by Kennard Ramphal

Cousin Ramadhin had a favorite red rooster which he raised from the moment it popped out of its shell. Over time, the rooster imprinted itself on Ramadhin and a steadfast bond developed between the bird and my cousin.

Whenever Ramadhin sat down to eat, either in the hammock, or sitting in one of the wooden chairs designed for the bottom house, the rooster strutted to him, and he would share his meal, dropping some rice or roti on the ground. When Ramadhin and the rooster first developed this relationship, the other chickens tried to approach him and partake of his offerings, but were vigorously shooed away. After a while, they did not even bother to approach our cousin, and left him to pamper his favorite rooster when he ate his roti or rice and fried or curried vegetables.

The rooster felt so safe that he slept on the lowest branch of the orange tree which was just outside the kitchen.

In spite of repeated objections from my mother, Daddy had bought a brand-new Morris Oxford, affectionately nicknamed, *The Bull*.

"You and them boys, gon just take the car to go and drink all over the place," she had said.

At sixteen, I was the youngest of *them boys*—my elder brothers being eighteen and twenty.

My father insisted that he and the boys will run the car private-hire, meaning that although it would be registered as a private car to save on insurance, we would run it as a hire-car, and bring in enough money to pay for the car and its upkeep.

One of our routines every Saturday night was attending *The Plaza*, a cinema located at Wales, and owned by Lee, who would let the driver of a car which brought patrons of the cinema from outlying areas, go to any section of the cinema free of charge. We would take a carload of as many as twelve people, including our cousin Ramadhin, and after dropping most of the passengers home, would go to the home of one of our friends to savor a bottle or two of El Dorado rum. Of course, after a few drinks, we would want something to eat. Meat was preferable, along with some boiled rice, and we would kill one of the chickens belonging to the owner of the house in which we found ourselves.

Noor was an expert in catching, killing, feathering, preparing and cooking the chickens, and he was a take-charge man who delegated responsibilities for who cooked the rice, and added the masala and garlic to the pot. His mantra was: "I don't need any knife. Too much blood," as he prepared to wring the neck of a chicken. Everybody appreciated his skills, and if the truth be told, that was the main reason why the group asked him to stick with us, when the other passengers were not invited.

We enjoyed this routine for several weeks, in spite of the several admonishments from Ma.

"I knew this would happen," she said. Then she turned to Daddy. "Before you buy the car, them boys gon go to Prag on Saturday, take a few drinks, and then come home. Now they take a whole clique to *The Plaza*, and then drink for most of the night. Next morning, they can't wake up."

On a moonlit Saturday night, the usual group went to see *Deedar* at The Plaza, and came back singing, *Bachapan Ka Dina Bhola Na Dena* out of tune all the way home. After dropping the passengers home, we stopped at Prag's Rum Shop, bought two bottles of El Dorado rum, and ended up in the kitchen at Ramadhin's house, for a drinking session.

Noor said, "If we going to kill a fowl, we better do it now, before we get too drunk. Remember last week, Ramadhin? You get so drunk that you couldn't eat the chicken we cook at Dhanraj place. Leh we start cooking the chicken now, so that we all can eat. Then if you get drunk, you can sleep. At least you got something in yuh stomach."

Ramadhin stopped humming *Bachapan Ka Dina Bhola Na Deena* and replied automatically, "You go and select any fowl, Noor. Deo, you know where the masala and everything is. Dhanraj can put on the rice to boil."

Noor left the kitchen and Ramadhin resumed humming the theme song from Deedar. After about forty seconds, he began to feel uneasy, but couldn't identify the specific reason. Suddenly, he remembered the rooster and sprang out of his chair. He bolted out of the kitchen, ignoring the drinks he spilled on the table. He saw Noor standing under the tree where the rooster slept, and he felt a bit relieved but when he glanced down, he saw his favorite rooster fluttering on the ground.

"Not that one," Ramadhin shouted frantically.

"See if it living," Noor replied, casually. "If it living, put it back on the branch."

Ramadhin glanced at the rooster and saw that the fluttering was abating. He cried,. "Not that one! Not that one!" was all he could say between sobs.

"Too late!" Noor replied, laconically. "You tell me to go and select any fowl. I done wring it neck."

"Not that one!" Ramadhin repeated, as he continued crying.

We all heard the interaction, and hustled outside, where Noor was attempting to put his arm around Ramadhin's shoulder to console him, and Ramadhin kept brushing it away. Then, Ramadhin suddenly broke away from the group and headed to the kitchen, when he poured half a tumbler of rum and drank it all in four gulps, while he sobbed intermittently.

That night, we had to make-do with a less rum, but we all had a bit more chicken, because while Ramadhin drank more than his share, he refused eat. In fact, he swore off chicken for an entire year.

"Not that one," he mumbled for the rest of our time together.

4 RIFLE AT THE READY by Ram Jagessar

One of the first groups I joined on entering the University of the West Indies (UWI)) was the Rifle Club and glad I was to do something forbidden to most Trinidadians.

We had an armoury with a handful of obsolete 303 rifles shooting .22 ammunition at a range near Piarco Airport. There were handguns too, used by the senior members. We newbies were not allowed to touch the pistols.

We did our firearm security lessons and the following day, five of us went for our first practice at the range. The senior Rifle Club student handed out a rifle to each man and warned that we were to keep it with us at all times and never to put it down any place away from us.

The only car available to take us to the range was a small four door beast, a Morris Oxford, that could barely hold the five of us. We squeezed in with our rifles and found we couldn't fit. Storing the rifles in the trunk was not an option, but the rifles could not fit in the car with us. We left for the range with five rifles sticking out three open windows.

When we reached the Airport Road, our driver cursed and said he was low on gas. Not a problem, as there was a gas station on the road before the range. Even better, the gas station was open. The driver pulled in beside a pump and looked around for the gas station attendant.

We were choked up in that hot car and every man jack came out for a breather. With our rifles slung over our shoulders, as ordered by the *Big Gun*, we walked around the station looking for the attendant. None appeared. The gas station office was also empty.

We all started walking around the gas station, calling for the attendant, and shouting some good-natured curses about his parentage, which I will not repeat.

After several minutes calling for the attendant with rifles on us as instructed, we noticed a young fellow peeping fearfully from the back of the office building.

"What are you doing back there, you lazy son of a bitch? Come and pump some gas for us," I shouted.

Gesturing for him to come forward and do his work didn't seem to work either. Eventually from the tone of our friendly insults and the fact that we were not pointing the guns at him, the attendant gingerly came out to pump our gas, ready to run at any threatening move from five armed looking bandits walking around his station.

Now we understood. When he saw five armed men coming out of the car, he thought that it was a robbery and he bolted to the back of the building where we couldn't see him. Only our friendly gestures and Trinidad style insults got him to emerge and pump our gas.

We thanked him and went on our way, oblivious to the spectacle of a car with five rifles sticking out the windows on the way to the airport.

5 ATHLETE'S FOOT by Roop Misir

One day I felt itches between my toes and noticed reddening around my feet's lower perimeter. They smelled putrid, and soon red lesions appeared. These became larger and started to spread in jagged lines– much like the receding foamy line of an ebbing wave on a sandy seashore. Before long, my feet would be covered with lesions. At least, that was what was going through my mind.

With each passing day, the lesions grew by a few millimeters, causing much concern, discomfort, and anxiety. Whenever I took off my shoes, the odour on my socks and feet was strong and repulsive. I dared not go to places like houses of worship and certain restaurants where I had to take off my shoes. Therefore, I needed to treat this infection urgently.

So, I consulted my physician, Dr Williams in Georgetown.

"You have athletes' foot," he said.

"But Doc," I explained, "I am not an athlete. Never do I have the time to play games, much less become an athlete."

He smiled cynically and explained to me as I would explain to a grade three student, "Your condition is caused by a fungus. Common skin infections like this one are also known as tinea infections. When the fungus grows on the feet, this condition is called Athlete's Foot—*Tinea pedicus*. Usually, it affects people whose feet tend to be damp and sweaty, which is often the case with athletes. However, anyone can get this infection, Mr. Misir. It's not restricted to athletes. Also, fungus infections can be serious. I've read of people with lung infections—aspergillosis—developing serious complications."

Then he added, "I've seen hundreds of cases before. The good news is that your foot condition is not as bad as some cases I've seen over the years." He then handed me a prescription for an ointment. "Go, fill it at your local drug store."

Dr. Williams didn't tell me the name of the prescription. Neither did I ask him. Other than physicians and pharmacists, only a few lay people could decipher the scrawls of the physician's Rx (prescription). It was as if it was in a foreign language—illegible to me.

When Dr. Williams saw me poring over the prescription with a puzzled look, he added, "The ointment contains cortisone. If your body can handle the cortisone, and you follow the instructions and apply the ointment as directed, your feet should clear up in a week or two. Make sure you wash your feet, and wipe them dry, especially between your toes. And always use a clean cloth."

Later that day, I decided to go to a local drugstore in Georgetown to have the Rx filled. I gave the pharmacist the Rx and had to wait for fifteen minutes. Then a courteous pharmacist assistant handed me the packaged ointment. "That would be seven dollars."

I was a bit surprised at the high price but decided to take it.

As I did recall, a few weeks before a friend had bought an over-the-counter athlete's foot ointment for $1.40, so I questioned why I should pay five times the price. Medicine prices must be increasing. However, I desperately wanted to get rid of this annoying fungal infection, so I paid for the ointment. Thankfully, my athlete's foot disappeared after one week.

As for the name of my previously filled prescription, I was able to decipher it the next day. It was Hydrocortisone ointment. Its over-the-counter price was 69 cents, less than a tenth of the seven dollars I paid.

Just as I was leaving, the same pharmacist assistant gave a newly filled prescribed medication to another customer. Then I overheard, "That would be forty-four dollars!"

Fumbling for words, the man reluctantly paid this exorbitant amount. He happened to be White, presumably a British expatriate. At that time, the starting salary for a pupil teacher was $45 a month. Which made me wonder why the man's prescription medicines would cost so much. Perhaps it had to do with the day-to-day politics at that time!

The time of my filling the prescriptions was 1962, and the political discourse in British Guiana was boiling over. Independence fever was in the air. Many former colonies had already gained political independence, and local politicians were agitating for the British rulers to quit and leave British Guiana. However, Mother Britain was making excuses, and using delaying tactics. These strategies no doubt induced fear among consumers and perhaps producers/suppliers as well, leading to supply chain disruptions and consequently high prices. Concurrently, there were food shortages, and wage and strict price controls. Suddenly, businesspeople were blamed for all kinds of problems. And British nationals were no longer welcome!

To me, over-the-counter pricing, but not higher costs of prescription, might be more reasonable. Prescription drug prices should reflect the cost of the drug plus the dispensing fee. Therefore, in a transparent marketplace, customers would know the prices before they pay. At this pharmacy, however, guidelines were not in place or followed, leaving the pharmacists to charge whatever they chose.

So while I got off rather lightly by paying only seven dollars, the expatriate Britisher paid what amounted to a king's ransom. This was not a tenable situation, I thought. I guess in times of seething unrest and ongoing uncertainty, all is fair in prescription drug pricing, versus the more attractive over-the-counter pricing.

Overcharging, or irrational pricing, might be as old as shopkeepers. Surely, it didn't start at my local drugstore, nor will it end there.

Across the world, the practice of market pricing is more the norm and is based on charging whatever the market would bear. When this system is used with ingenuity, can potentially turn savvy investors into billionaires!

In the case of prescribed drug pricing at the local level, what's needed is to practice a more humane version of capitalism, one with clear guidelines. Ethics, fairness, and transparency can strike a harmonious balance for both the customer and businesses alike. What needs to be preserved is the free-market goose that lays the golden egg.

And just as the miracle of hydrocortisone cleared up my athlete's foot infection, no doubt the realistic pricing of essential prescribed medication would be a win-win relationship for both sides, minimizing ridiculous medicine hyperinflation, or *Medflation*.

6 PLAYING COW by Kennard Ramphal

"I can't find the ball," Jairam shouted to Seegol. The two friends were playing a variation of cricket on the deserted road in front of their house.

One-tip, two-tip, is a game in which you have to run when you hit the ball two times. It was a popular game when only two or three players were available, because batters could be out more easily than in regular games when batters could blot the ball indefinitely. It was Friday afternoon and half of the sun was still visible in the west, so there was enough light to play.

Jairam delivered a pitch and the ball bounced just before it reached Seegol, giving him an opportunity to hit it in a clump of bushes littered with fallen leaves. After running the length of the makeshift cricket pitch, a garbage can at one end to serve as a wicket, and an upturned rusty bucket to mark the bowler's spot, Seegol joined Jairam in the futile search for the ball, which was their last one. After nearly an hour, they were tired and frustrated, and their shirts were wet with sweat. A sponge ball cost eighty-five cents at Inderdai's Store, and neither of them had money to buy another one.

Both friends were wondering what they should do in the fading late afternoon light and the limited time they had left.

"The ball done lost," Seegol observed. "Tomorrow, we can search for it again, but it too early for me to go home. Wha' we gon do?"

Jairam scratched his head, furiously thinking of something fun he could do with his friend. Then he remembered how fascinated he was by the sound their cow made after it was branded by their father the previous day. He had tried to imitate the sounds, but acknowledged that he could not, and he admired Seegol's ability to imitate not only other people's speech, but also the sounds made by animals, including various birds. He remembered that the branding iron was still lying outside the cow shed on the ashes of the fire his father had lit.

"Let we play cow," Jairam told his friend.

"Wha' you mean?" Seegol replied, "A cow just eat grass all day. Me mother cook good dahl and roti, and you want me to eat grass."

"Yesterday, me father brand our cow, and it make a funny sound. Like this! Maaahaaa! No, I can't do it."

"I bet I can," Seegol boasted. "Remember when I stutter just like Teacher Sugrim. Dhanraj was pissing near cricket pitch, and when I say D-D-Dhanraj, you got n-n-n-no s-s-shame, he cut he piss and nearly shit he pants?"

Jairam laughed loudly as he remembered the incident. Although he admired Seegol's ability to mimic the sounds of animals, he doubted whether his friend could imitate the sound of a cow after it was branded. "I bet you can't holler like a cow when it has been branded," he challenged.

"I can make any sound that I want. God give me that power," Seegol boasted.

"All right! Let me bring the branding iron, and I gon press it against you backside and leh we see if you can holler like our cow."

Seegol got down on all fours and Jairam pressed the cold branding iron against his haunches.

"Baaaaa!" Seegol shouted.

"Cows don't go Baaaaa! You ever her cow holler like a sheep? You didn't feel the iron because you got yuh pants on."

Seegol looked around, and seeing nobody around, dropped his pants and Jairam pressed the cold branding iron against his haunch. "Meeeeee!" Seegol screamed.

"It useless, Seegol. You can talk like some people and make sounds like some animals. But you can't holler like a cow when you brand it."

Seegol angrily replied, "What do you mean? Listen to this." Seegol made sounds like a *kiskadee*.

Even though Jairam knew that it was his friend who made the sound, it was so real that he found himself looking up in the trees, searching for a kiskadee. "You hear kiskadee making kiss-ka-deee sound many time. How many time you hear cow make sound when they get brand?"

"You right! I hear the sound cow make when they get brand one or two time. But you know me? Lemme think about it and tomorrow you gon see. I gon holler just like cow. I gon come about two o'clock."

When Seegol left Jairam, he racked his brains to recollect the sound of a branded cow. He remembered when he saw Heera's cow being branded, and tried to recollect the sounds it made. He played the sounds repeatedly in his mind, until he was sure that he could mimic it. To be certain, he practiced the sound quietly that night before he went to bed.

The following day was a hot one, and the sun was shining brightly when Seegol confidently made his way to Jairam's house just before two o'clock. Jairam had spent the morning picking coffee beans with his mother and the girls she had hired. Although he enjoyed being with the girls, he remembered his appointment with Seegol, and was about one hundred yards from his house when he saw Seegol walking across the bridge leading to his house.

"I got it down, pat," Seegol shouted when his friend was about twenty yards away. "Leh we try it right away."

Jairam left his water bottle and his cutlass on the steps of his house, and went directly to the cow shed, where Seegol, anxious to show off his prowess, had already dropped his pants, and was crouching on all fours. As Jairam picked up the branding iron, he noticed some smoke rising from the ashes, but thought nothing of it, as he pressed the iron against Seegol's haunch.

"Owwww!" Seegol shouted, and started jumping up and down. A strange smell assaulted Jairam's nostrils, but he was too focused on Seegol's antics to pay any attention to it.

"Cow don't holler Owww," Jairam told Seegol, who jumped into the four-foot drain and sat down in the water. "And cow don't do that," he continued.

"The iron hot, you rass. You burn me."

Jairam's father, hearing Seegol's screams, came out of the house. "Why Seegol hollering?" he asked his son.

"I pretend to brand him so that he can holler like our cow when you brand it, but he say that the iron hot."

"Jaigobin brought his cow for me to brand because he too cheap to pay to get he own brand. So, I brand his cow and left the brand on the fire. I didn't know that you and Seegol stupid enough to play cow and brand one another. Seegol, come out of the four-foot[1] and let me see the brand."

When Seegol came out of the water, he would not show Jairam's father or Jairam, who was wondering whether the brand would look the same as it did on cows. From that day on, Seegol's friends missed him when they went swimming naked at the conservancy.

Everybody in the village started calling Seegol, "Cow," and the younger children never knew his real name. When he got married, even his wife called him, "Cow."

Years later, when he passed away, two men rode through the village on a bicycle ringing a bell and shouting, "COW DEAD! FUNERAL TOMORROW AT FOUR O'CLOCK!"

---

[1] A trench about four feet deep

7 THE ANGUILLA DEMONSTRATION by Ram Jagessar

It was a warm tropical day in March 1969 when I joined a band of hot-headed radicals from the University of the West Indies in Trinidad to demonstrate in front of the British High Commission in the capital city, Port Of Spain. Every day was a warm tropical day in Trinidad, but no matter.

Britain had done wrong to the 1,739 black people from the tiny Caribbean island of Anguilla who had declared their independence from the tiny twin island colony of St Kitts and Anguilla. The British envoy who came to Anguilla to tell the 1,739 black people they had to accept White British rule again was expelled from the island. He called for help and a British parachute regiment came in, and expelled the Anguilla republic from existence.

Black people in the university were infuriated at this colonial brutality, and screamed that the evil White imperialists had done it again to the black man. Various radical hotheads like me were also angry enough to drop our books and go down to Port of Spain to let Britain know we wouldn't take it. I myself never missed a student demonstration or any demonstration if I could help it.

That's how I came to witness the international incident that never happened at the Anguilla demonstration.

We gathered in front of the British High Commission on Independence Square in the blazing sun that morning. About two hundred angry young people were waving placards and screaming slogans against the British. Police had blocked off traffic on the road, so we were nicely positioned like a swarm of wasps in front of the High Commission door.

After a fiery speech that drew much applause and insults hurled at the British, our leader shouted into his bullhorn that the High

Commissioner should come outside and accept a protest note to the British government. The crowd buzzed like a disturbed Jack Spaniard nest and screamed its support. The police looked on from the background, but did not attempt to stop our demonstration.

After a while a representative from the British High Commission came out. I think it was the High Commissioner himself. This White man in his dark blue suit came out the door, pipe firmly in his teeth, and looked out at the crowd of demonstrators. All he could see was a mob of mostly young black men shouting, and screaming with rage. We stood between him and our leader with the bullhorn about 100 metres away, clearly blocking his way. He hesitated.

Our leader saw the problem at once and asked us to make way for the British representative to come up and accept the protest letter. The crowd opened up to form a narrow passageway from the High Commission's door where he was standing, straight to our leader with the letter and the bullhorn.

The White man in the dark suit walked out calmly and slowly into that furious crowd of demonstrators stacked up three or more deep. The noise was deafening. That crowd hated the man and all he represented and you could feel their rage in the air and on the ground. He went straight up, took the protest letter from our leader, and said in a clear, firm voice that he would convey it to the proper authorities.

Then he turned around and walked slowly back towards the High Commission door. The crowd exploded again in a deafening roar, but the man did not seem to hear any of it. His pipe never wavered. His hand never trembled. He seemed to be walking in slow motion as if he was strolling along Mayaro Beach. It was what they call a surreal moment that you hear about so often but very rarely experience.

As he went back, the crowd closed in around him in the most menacing manner conceivable. I was standing halfway to the High Commission door, with about two people in front of me and the narrowing corridor that the White man was walking through. His was the only white face in that crowd of black and brown enemies.

A big Black man in front of me had been one of the angriest of the noise makers, and he had shouted himself hoarse in the protest. I don't remember anything about him except that he was big and he was really, really angry, about one step short of foaming at the mouth. He was in the front row of the corridor, and behind him was another Black man and then me.

When the High Commissioner moved past directly in front of him, the big Black man exploded. I saw him pull back his right hand to hit the High Commissioner who was passing by not more than three feet away. I said to myself, he's going to cuff down the ambassador! If he hits him, the crowd will tear that White man to pieces right here and now. An international incident is happening right in front of me, and nothing can stop it.

But I had forgotten the other Black man in front of me and directly behind the big Black man about to attack the High Commissioner. He was made of better stuff. He grabbed the attacker's right arm when he pulled it back to strike, and held on to the arm. The High Commissioner walked back to the door and disappeared inside.

The Commissioner had seen nothing, and neither had anybody else except the man behind the attacker and me. We both remained frozen in another of those surreal moments, while the crowd turned around and dispersed. As far as I know, nobody said or wrote anything about this incident. After all, it never happened.

To this day more than forty years later I still remember that British High Commissioner with undiminished admiration. I don't care for Britain or British actions in Anguilla at the time, but that White man in the dark suit is the bravest man I've ever seen. If I were in his shoes, nothing in the world could have gotten me to walk into that mob that day.

8 HOW I CAME TO STUDY SCIENCE by Roop Misir

When I attended Primary school in the 1950s in British Guiana, we had no option. We had to study a limited number of subjects offered, including English, Arithmetic, Geography, and smatterings of Hygiene, plus History about European conquests and domination worldwide. As compared to what we now know in 2022, knowledge then was elementary. And even though expanding, it was still a drop in the ocean.

Subjects were focused on Eurocentrism, and their delivery was Anglo-centric, designed to transform us heathens into docile citizens. Our Hindu Indian civilization and culture were completely ignored or presented as primitive and barbaric, our menfolk as meek and weak, and women as uneducated, stupid, and designed merely as objects of pleasure and baby-making machines. Hindi and other Indian languages were never offered. One way to break a people would be to deprive them of their language and culture. And this was covertly done. The entire agenda seemingly so very painlessly that before long, we'd grown to hate ourselves and love the British!

Then one day, I decided to take a closer look at my imaginary crystal ball. And suddenly, my *Quo Vadis* moment dawned.

In the new world order, the future of humankind lay in science and spinoffs in technology—its applications to the manufacture of products. This very notion presented exciting new opportunities so intriguing that I was determined to study the relevant science subjects. And later, to ensure every student at school was included, I did make the case for co-education in schools by writing an essay, entitled: *Should Boys and Girls be Educated Together*? To say the least, my teachers were very proud of my boldness!

Some years later, this dream was realized when all schools were designated as coeducational institutions, including the elite schools: Queen's College (Boys) and Bishops High School (Girls).

Having imbued the rudiments of science education at the primary level, my study of science was in abeyance for many years, necessitated by my helping Pa work full time at the rice fields. For one whole year thereafter, I was apprenticed to a local motor mechanic at the neighboring village of La Jalousie, WCD. Mr. George had promised to pay me $1 per day. However, he overworked both me and another boy from 7 AM-6 PM. He never paid us a single red cent, but enriched himself in the process.

Pa was publicly shamed by family, neighbours and village elders. This propelled Pa to get me out of this pseudo-apprenticeship. That was the turning point.

My fellow village elders and relatives offered encouragement. As well, former teachers kept reminding me to come back to school. Pa finally listened to the court of public opinion. He agreed to re-register me at St. Anthony's Anglican School. Here, I was exposed to the principles of grammar and the basics of science. Later that year, I passed the Primary School Leaving Examination and received the Primary School Certificate. That was the beginning!

My salvation was my love of reading. Success at school won the admiration of my teachers, who all insisted that Pa send me to a secondary school in Georgetown—the sky was the limit.

Ours was a large family, poor and struggling to make ends meet. Then I reminded Pa of a saying I read in the textbook, The Student's Companion. *Where there's a will there's a way.*

I was determined to study there. There and then, I realized that if I must be in classes with fellow students my age, my learning curve must be near vertical, not slowly inclining conventionally. And so, in just one year of self-directed study, I taught myself Latin and Health Sciences, etc. For much of my relaxation time, I would immerse myself daily in our ancient inspirational masterpieces: *The Bhagavad Gita* and *The Holy Ramayana*. Remarkably, I passed the Senior Cambridge Certificate Examination. This so emboldened me that I set my sights on bigger and better achievements.

My formal high School years happened to coincide with the turbulent years (1961-64) when foreign-engineered unrest catalyzed widespread riots and polarized our country along racial lines.

Despite setbacks, I survived and thrived. Success bred more success. During the following years, I was able to attend high schools, notably Indian Educational Trust College. Here I was exposed to some of the best teachers, notably Mr. Akbar Ali (Mathematics, the language of science) and also Messrs. Havildar Singh (Biology), Kapildev Prashad (Chemistry), and Narendra Nath (Physics). All these fine teachers took an interest in helping me understand new concepts. It was noteworthy that I entered high school, starting in Form 5, not Form 3 as would have been the case normally. This enabled me to study for GCE science subjects. Because I didn't have the luxury of leisure and time. Whatever I had to do, I had to do it—fast!

After excelling in the GCE *O* levels exams, I served as a teacher of science subjects at my former Primary School, and later at the Zeeburg Government Secondary School, West Coast Demerara (WCD). It was noteworthy that concurrently I studied at the University of Guyana (UG), which offered evening classes (Queen's College campus). My course of study was science: Biology (major) and Chemistry (minor). As it turned out, my classmate, neighbor, and friend was former Queen's College alumnus Joseph G. Singh, later the Chief of Staff, Guyana Defence Force.

In 1973, I came to Canadian universities to pursue Higher studies in Animal Science (BSA 1975, MSc 1977, Manitoba, and PhD 1982, Alberta). Naturally, these degrees coupled with my post-doctoral fellowship prepared me for a career in scientific research and teaching. I've had the privilege to live and serve in the prairie provinces, of Manitoba, Alberta, and Saskatchewan.

My wife and family wanted to live closer to relatives, most of whom lived in eastern Canada—Ontario and Quebec. So, we migrated from the West and came to Toronto (1986). Here I chose to return to teaching Science at the Collegiate, retiring in 2010.

Yes, my study of science was well worth the effort, paving the way for a lifetime of friendship, work, and achievement.

These days (2023), the rate of increase in knowledge is exponential. The sky is the limit!

9 THE CRICKET MATCH by Kennard Ramphal

Canal No. 2 Polder had two cricket teams. Sports Cricket Club played in the cricket field behind the school, while Cultural Cricket Club played in a cricket field behind Buddy Boy's cake shop. Buddy Boy's cake shop was the cultural center of *Bottom Side*—the area east of Manbahal's rum shop, to the conservancy Canal which marked the eastern boundary of the village. The community center, which was located just beside the school, was the hub of *Top Side*, the area from west of Manbahal to Stanleytown, the village west of Canal No. 2.

The rivalry between the Cultural Cricket Club and the Sports Cricket Club was fierce, and many of their supporters got into heated arguments, and indeed fights, while defending the merits of the two teams.

My family lived about half a mile east of Manbahal, and were therefore residents of *Bottom Side*. While my two older brothers and I supported the Cultural Cricket Club, we were also very invested in ourselves, and decided to form our own club, although we were not even average cricket players.

Behind our house was a grassy patch—ideal for a miniature cricket field. Cricket beckoned, and we answered. We cleared the ground for a cricket pitch and cut six relatively straight branches for wickets. With our pocketknives, we carved grooves on the top of the wickets and put small sticks on the top to act as bails. My eldest brother, John, had liberated some white chalk from his classroom, and we used it to mark the creases. However, we decided that, as professionals, we could not skimp on the bat and ball, so we bought one bat, autographed by Don Bradman, a red Supreme County Game cricket ball with prominent seams to accommodate Andrew's spin bowling, and a pair of pads from Bookers Store.

A cricket team is made up of at least eleven players, and we managed to convince eight young men, who were not good enough to play with either the Cultural or the Sports Cricket Clubs, to join us.

At that time, cricket mania swept Guyana, including our village, because Australia was touring the West Indies, and people identified themselves not only with particular teams, but with individual players. To call a batsman, "Rohan Kandhai" was the greatest compliment you could give him. John, Abel and I were not good enough for people to name us after famous players, so we named ourselves. I called myself Richie Benaud, after the Australian batsman. John, who had a unique style of batting because the movement of his bat was followed by a sweep of his pad, providing double protection—against the rules of cricket, called himself Rohan Kanhai. The great batsman would not have been flattered that someone with John's batting style would be presumptuous enough to adopt his name. Abel, who could hit the wicket two times out of six when he bowled his slow pitch, called himself Garfield Sobers.

Our cricket field was confined by necessity, because coffee trees surrounded it, and we had to set our boundaries about twenty feet from the wickets. This meant that a batsman had to *blot* a ball past the fielders to earn four runs. Very often, we would spend over half an hour searching for the ball among the fallen leaves of the coffee trees. In this situation, who would not feel good about himself after making sixty runs, when Kanhai made a mere fifty? Even our team as a whole felt good. I remembered our team making two hundred and fifty-one runs in one innings, when the West Indies made a measly two hundred and twenty.

Sooklall lived in Stanley Town, a village at the junction of the Canal Road and the West Bank Road, and he came through Canal every afternoon with his donkey cart, selling crushed ice, topped with sweet syrup. In the hot tropical climate, children and adults considered their five cents well spent in exchange for a cup of crushed ice and syrup.

When my two brothers and I went to buy ice from Sooklall one afternoon, John boasted, "I made ninety-one runs today."

"You are a good batsman," Sooklall responded. "Which cricket team you belong to?"

John hesitated for a few seconds before he responded, "Oh, we haven't named it yet. We want to play other teams." John, of course, knew the two teams in Canal, but was not foolish enough to challenge them.

Sooklall stopped shaving ice for a while, and looked at John. "The boys in the Stanleytown Cricket Club are looking to play another team for practice. You want me to arrange a match for you?"

We had never heard of the Stanleytown Cricket Club, although I rode through Stanleytown every weekday, because I had to pass through that village in order to get to Wales School, where I taught. I was quite certain that they were also not aware of the existence of our cricket club, and we were eager to demonstrate our skills.

"Yes," John eagerly told him. "We can come next week."

"I will tell the boys, and see if they can play next week," Sooklall responded while he shaved the last cup of ice for us. As he poured the thick syrup in the cup of ice he told John, "You and your team will have a good match."

We were on summer holidays, and every day after breakfast, we found ourselves on our cricket field, where we practiced until the sun got too hot. Then we went inside and did some reading or writing, until it got cooler, and we were able to resume our practice.

"You all stop studying for your exam?" Ma admonished, when she noticed the amount of time we spent on our cricket field.

"The exam not until next June," John replied. "Plenty of time to study."

"Summer holiday is the only time all of you can be together," she observed. "You can help each other study."

"You never knew that you had three sons who are great cricket players," John bragged. "We have our own cricket team now. We named it John's Cricket Club."

It was the first time Abel and I had heard the name of our cricket club, but we accepted it unquestioningly, because we often found it useless to argue with our eldest brother.

Ma gave us an indulgent smile, and went about her business, after advising us, "All right! Play your cricket, but study too. Is education make you become teachers, not cricket."

Normally, we would buy *crush-ice* two or three times a week, but we found ourselves waiting for Sooklall every day after he promised to arrange the match. On the Monday of the following week, Sooklall found John, Abel, and myself anxiously waiting for him, each of us with a cup in one hand, and five cents in the other.

As he shaved the ice for us, Sooklall addressed John, who had nominated himself captain of the team. "Dem boys got the pitch smooth like a billiard table for you. You guys gon come on Sunday?"

"Sunday is good," John told him. "We gon come to start at eleven o'clock."

"Australia and the West Indies start at eleven o'clock. Ah gon tell them boys to expect you at eleven."

John then remembered that our cricket club owned only a bat. a ball and a pair of pads. "We just formed our club," he told Sooklall. "We don't have much gear. Dem boys got cricket gear?"

"Yes, you can borrow their gear," Sooklall reassured us. "Just don't let them boys wait for you and you don't show up."

John squared his shoulders and held his right-hand shoulder high, with his palm facing outwards. "My word is my bond," he proclaimed. "We gon come at about ten, so that we can start at eleven."

We puffed out our chests, and strutted away, savoring our shaved-ice and syrup.

John, Abel, and I intensified our practice, along with the other team members who were naïve enough to join us, and we set out on Sunday with our one bat, one ball, a pair of pads, and high hopes. When our team, dressed in a motley array of shirts and trousers, arrived at the cricket field behind Stanleytown Elementary School, we met the members of the opposing team, all dressed in white suits, with only two of them wearing floppy cricket hats.

We were immediately disoriented when we saw the regulation size cricket field, which, of course, was much larger than ours, but we endeavored to hide our nervousness.

After the usual pleasantries, John and the other captain, Edmund Manifold, a tall six-footer who was teaching in Stanleytown School, and the umpire, John Mansfield, who was the headmaster of the same school, went to the cricket pitch for the toss. The umpire tossed a penny in the air, and John confidently called, *Heads*! The penny fell on *Tails*, and Stanleytown Cricket Team elected to bat first.

John selected me as the opening bowler. He was the wicket keeper, Abel was in the fine slip, and the other members of the team were allotted their respective positions. My first pitch to the opening batter was hit for a six. Undaunted, I bowled the second pitch, which was way off the wicket to the leg side of the batter, who was merciful, and hit it only for a four. I gave up one more six, and two fours in that over, and was relieved when it was concluded.

John assigned me to keep square slip while Bayo bowled. He fared better than I did, giving up only one six, and two fours in the over. I was surprised when John asked me to bowl again, after exhorting me to, "Hit the batter if you can't hit the wicket."

I aimed the first delivery at the pad of the batter, who hit the ball which ricocheted off his pad, and bounced to the wicket. When the umpire raised his hand, I was flushed with success, and aimed all my deliveries to the batter's pad. The strategy was no longer successful, and my deliveries were hit either for a four or a six.

The second *Out* we were able to achieve was when the ball was nicked by the batter, and John managed to hold on to it. Stanleytown *declared*[2] when they were ninety-one for two. It was our turn to bat.

John and I were the opening batsmen, and John faced the first delivery of the fast bowler, a huge player with rippling biceps. He confidently tried the bat and pad technique, and there was a loud appeal from the bowler as the ball resounded against his pad, which was directly in front of the wicket. The umpire pointed to the sky

---

[2] Decided not to bat any more, although all their team members did not bat.

with his index finger, and John gave a perplexed look, because nobody would dare to call him out when he played with us. However, he recognized the futility of any objection in the present situation, and reluctantly made his way to the shaded area behind the school which served as a pavilion.

The next batter, Sunkand, survived two delivers, simply because he did not swing the bat and the ball bounced an inch or two off the top of the wickets. He was not so lucky on the third delivery, and the ball picked off the bails so neatly that the wickets remained upright. The bowler appealed and the umpire put up his hand. When Sunkand looked back and saw that the wickets were undisturbed, he could not understand what was happening, and refused to leave the wicket until the fielder from the fine slip retrieved the bails, went to Sunkand, and opening his hands, revealed the bails to him. Two outs and only four deliveries in the first over.

My hopes were not bright as Ramadhin, our cousin who lived opposite the school, and therefore was in Sports Club turf, but whom we coerced into joining our team, went to the wicket. A loud shout went up from our team as he managed to blot the ball back to the bowler. Although no run was scored, he showed us that we could at least defend the wicket against this team. My hopes of Ramadhin scoring a run on the last delivery of the over, so that I would not have to bat, went in the way of the bails flying in the dust. However, Ramadhin returned to the pavilion a hero, because he was the only batsman who managed to establish contact with the ball so far.

As I looked at the fast bowler getting ready for his delivery, I remembered our friendly cricket pitch, and just as I was comparing it to the gigantic monster of the field in which we were playing, the bowler delivered. I did not have an opportunity to move my bat, when the wickets went tumbling. John Mansfield knew me, and would have liked to give me a break, I imagined. Had it been an LBW[3], or even a nicked ball, he could have shaken his head for a *No*, but there was no denying an *Out* when my stumps were all scattered behind the crease. Instead of putting his hand up for an out, he turned to Edgar Manifold, and told him, "Give him another

---

[3] Leg Before Wicket: when the batsman either deliberately or unintentionally blocked the ball which would surely have hit the wicket.

at bat." Edgar Manifold was not going to argue with his headmaster, and nodded to the bowler, who took the ball and went to the spot he had designated as the starting point for his approach.

I was determined to make contact as the bowler released the ball. And I did! The ball rose about ten feet in the air, and was deftly caught by the fielder on the offside. Again, the umpire had no choice but to call me out. I half expected John Mansfield to say again, "Give him another bat," but he did not, and I remained at the wicket until he came and gently led me off the field. "You are a good teacher," he consoled.

The remainder of the team did not fare much better, although we did manage to score nine runs, four of them from *byes*, when the wicket keeper missed the ball and it went all the way to the boundary.

Edgar Manifold wanted to give us *two-for-one*[4] and sent us in to bat again. We did slightly better than we did in the first innings, and when we scored fifteen runs, all out, Edgar Manifold turned to his team and asked, "Should we give them *Three for one?*"

"Nah!" the wicket keeper, who was upset because he did not get an opportunity to bat, exclaimed. "We had enough fun for today."

Members of John's Cricket Club joined two hire cars and went home in silence. On the way home, I gave a great deal of thought to the humiliating defeat which we suffered, and rationalized that Stanleytown Cricket Club, like John's Cricket Club, was a new club, with Sooklall as its unofficial manager. Sooklall was wise enough not to match the team with a strong team at the beginning, but like the manager of a novice boxer, he matched it with a team which would ensure an easy victory. How he recognized John's Cricket Team as a team which could be easily beaten was anybody's guess.

When we arrived home, although Ma knew we had lost by taking one look at our faces, she asked John, "How the match go?"

John did not answer, perhaps because he wanted to spare Ma the extent of out humiliation. Instead, he turned to me and Abel, "You

---

[4] When one team bats two times and still cannot beat the score of the opposing team which batted once

know how much para-grass we can grow on that piece of land? We won't have to go to other people's land to cut grass for our cow."

Ma consoled us immediately. "The three of you very bright. Look at all the exam you pass."

John stood a bit taller. "Ma, you know that none of we ever failed an exam yet?"

"God bless me to have bright children," Ma said, as she lowered her head, and clasped her hands.

"They say that the more you put into Shakespeare, the more you get out of him. Leh we read *Merchant of Venice* again," John told me and Abel, as he went to the pile of books on the table.

Neither Abel nor I replied. We were too humiliated to concentrate on Shakespeare, as we tried to forget our first and last cricket match.

10 FLYING LESSONS by Ram Jagessar

Happily riding my beloved Honda 350 motorcycle along Independence Square in Port of Spain, I never expected to take to the air.

As I went past Columbus Square, I observed a road intersection coming up, with no stop signs in either direction. A motor car was coming down from my right about a hundred metres away. Not a problem! I had way enough time to go through the intersection before the car came up. Motor bikes are fast, and we bike men don't stop even for red lights.

I cranked the accelerator to get more speed and the bike leapt forward as expected and then coughed and dropped speed sharply. The gas to the carburetor had choked up, but I still had time to stop before the oncoming car on my right went through the intersection.

Then to my horror, the bike coughed again, as gas raced past the block into the engine, and the bike leaped right into the path of the oncoming car.

The front wheel of my bike soundlessly hit the left front fender of the car about six inches behind the headlight. The bike catapulted over the car and dropped about 20 feet on the other side of the car and out of the intersection. I also catapulted head over heels over the car. I thought I did.

Time went into slow motion or fast forward. I saw or heard nothing. It was a perfect moment in time. Or rather an imperfect moment in time.

I landed on my back 30 feet away, my helmet resting on the concrete curb. Not a cut or bruise, nor even a scratch on my red and white helmet.

For what felt like minutes, but were probably seconds, I got up without help and looked sadly at my bike on its side with the front wheel bent into a V standing on a round pizza with several slices missing. A split second more and the car would have slammed into my bike sideways, crushed my right leg and probably killed me. Two split seconds more and the bike would have slammed into the side of the car and me into the side of the car as well. Another motorcycle casualty.

I was young, in my twenties, and a motor-bike rider, and therefore was completely unfazed by the incident at the time.

We see *Yamraj* the God of death every week.

11 THE PILLION RIDER by Roop Misir

Ma, Pa, and two of my siblings once attended a social event at Mausi[5] Rajo's home in Canal No 1 Polder, West Bank Demerara. It was getting past 4 p.m., so Pa decided to return home to feed the milch cows we kept in our backyard at Windsor Forest, West Coast Demerara.

It was approaching 5 p.m. when he requested that I give him a ride home on my new Honda motorcycle. He had never ridden on a motorcycle before, but this time he was happy to be the pillion rider. So, after bidding relatives farewell, Pa joined me by the roadside where I was waiting for him.

CRASH COURSE

Ever since I could recall, Pa always had a bicycle. He would ride to various places along the coast, and at times cycle his way to catch the ferry from Vreed-en-hoop to Georgetown. He was accustomed to a muscle-pedaled bicycle with full control of direction and speed. This time though, it was different. He would be merely the pillion rider.

Before we started the journey home, the first thing I did was to give him a crash course on safety, and how to sit behind me on the saddle during the ride.

I demonstrated as I told him, "I will start the bike. Then you will sit on the seat, and keep your feet on the foot rack, holding on tight to the sides of the seat."

After sitting on the bike and starting it, I asked Pa to get on board. Anxious to get home, he eagerly mounted the seat behind me.

---

[5] Aunt in Hindi

"Understand?"

"Yes," he assured me.

Faithfully, he followed my instructions. I made sure he was sitting, grasping the sides of the seat, ready for the takeoff.

"Then here we go!"

THE RIDE

I drove for 100 yards, then made a brief stop. "How do you like the ride so far?" I inquired.

He gleefully exclaimed, "Great!"

"OK, then this time, I will be riding a little faster."

At La Grange village where the Canal Road East had a near 90-degree turn to connect with the West Bank Road en-route to Vreed-en-hoop, I made sure I slowed down before resuming my speed again. Everything was going well.

As happy as a lark, I inquired, "How is it going Pa?"

"Good so far. But sometimes when you turn a corner, I would lean to the opposite side. This way, I could remain straight up, and maintain my balance on the bike seat."

"Don't do this. Not good! Next time just sit still. Otherwise, you will fall off. Just go with the bike. Bank the road!"

"OK, I'll try."

From Vreed-en-hoop, we headed west along the West Coast Road for the last leg on the way home. For the next two miles, the road was straight, so I decided to accelerate the speed to 35-40 miles per hour. Thus far, Pa was holding on quite well. Just ahead of us was a sharp turn, followed by another in quick succession. And as before, I slowed down.

HAYNES TURN AND THE RESCUE

Heading towards Haynes Turn, I had to be cautious. This was

the infamous turn where many a road accident had occurred over the years. Sad to say, some of the accidents were fatal. The approach was clear so I speeded up. Instinctively, I was banking the turn, this time a bit faster. Pa got scared and forgot to lean into the turn. Instead, he tried to sit up and lean to the other side, just the opposite of what we agreed. As a consequence, I quickly lost control of the steering.

Splash!

The bike headed straight into the roadside ditch. Both of us were immersed in the nearly three feet of swampy water. I was confused and Pa was deeply embarrassed.

Ramjeet, an acquaintance for many years, lived nearby. He saw the incident as it unfolded, and quickly came to our rescue. He and Kishore quickly pulled a frightened, shivering Pa from the ditch. With some help, I managed to drag my motorcycle out of the water. Drenched in mud, its handlebar was twisted 30° to the left.

We both expressed our sincere thanks to our rescuers. On seeing Pa, a surprised Ramjeet said, "Chacha[6], how come you decided to be a pillion rider on the motorcycle? You would never sit even on a moving tractor!"

The silence was deafening. Then eventually Pa talked about geeing[7] grass to his hungry cows because they hadn't eaten since lunchtime.

Ramjeet chimed in. "Then come let me help you out. You must be cold. I'll bring you a towel and some clothes!"

Quickly he brought a brand-new extra-large towel and a new set of clothes. I was touched by his respect and kindness!

Then Ramjeet inquired, "What happened Roop?"

I explained, "Just an unfortunate accident. I'm very happy the accident was not very serious. No fractures, only a few scrapes, but we got dripping wet. The motorcycle isn't wrecked. It can be washed, fixed, and made new again. I am so sorry Pa's first pillion

---

[6] Uncle
[7] giving

riding ended in disaster."

BLISSFULLY HAPPY

Ramjeet smiled widely. "Now, we count our blessings and celebrate this event with a drink for you both. And Chacha, here's a very special drink that warms the body as it wakes you up!"

"Thank you." Then I started sipping my drink.

However, Pa gulped his drink all in one shot, and told Ramjeet, "Very refreshing!"

So, when Ramjeet offered him another drink, he welcomed it with pleasure. It was only when I noticed that both of us got the refreshing drink from the same decanter that I began to wonder

Did Ramjeet overstep his hospitality by offering Pa—a practicing pandit, rum and cola? Surely, I detected the taste of my favorite dark one with cola!

As it turned out, Pa was blissfully happy.

12 A LESSON IN PHYSICS by Kennard Ramphal

On an overcast Saturday afternoon in the rural village of Canal Number Two Polder, my elder brother, Abel, and I were studying for our teachers' exams for most of the day. At about four o'clock, Abel put down his book, and turned to me, his brown eyes unwavering, as if he was still concentrating on the events in British history he was just reading about. Looking at his intense facial features, I understood why he had the reputation for having an almost photographic memory.

Lean and wiry, Abel was eighteen months older than I, but we grew up as if we were twins, and wrote the Pupil Teachers' Appointment Examination, and almost all the other teachers' examinations, together.

"This is nice duck weather. Ducks always come to the mango trees just by the edge of that swamp behind our farm. We studied enough for today. Let's go and see if we can shoot a Muscovy duck or two."

I certainly needed no prompting. After teaching the whole week and studying all Saturday, I was feeling listless and bored, and had to frequently force myself to concentrate.

"Let's go!" I replied. "We can continue studying tomorrow, when we are fresh."

We closed our books, feeling satisfied that we put in almost a full day of study. After we changed into the clothes we wore to work in the farm, which we called *Back-dam clothes*, we put on our worn-out sneakers, and set out with our father's sixteen-bore shotgun and six cartridges.

We envied the people who could walk barefoot, because the thick calluses on the soles of their feet protected their feet from thorns. We were required to wear shoes as teachers, and the soles of our feet were quite soft, making it unthinkable for us to go to the farm, or to the jungle without any footwear.

The sun was partially hidden by clouds, and the air was laden with moisture, but Abel and I were not concerned about getting wet. We welcomed the rain as we walked along the path between the coffee trees laden with red coffee berries. We wanted to show anybody who saw us that, although we were teachers, we were as rough and tough as the other youths in the village.

"Ducks like to feed at dusk," Abel reminded me, "and they like wet weather. Today looks like a good day for them."

"The number five cartridges we have are good for ducks," I observed. "But this time when we shoot the duck, let's go right away and find it while it's still stunned from the fall. Remember the time when we shot a duck as it was flying, and we spent so much time congratulating each other, that when we went to pick the duck up, we found that it was only wounded, and it hid so well in the swamp that we couldn't find it, and had to go home empty-handed?"

Abel laughed as he remembered the incident. "You were the one who wanted me to congratulate you on your good shot, otherwise we would have gotten the duck," he reminded me.

I acknowledged my fault for the delay in retrieving the duck. Although we were extremely upset at that time for not getting it, we found that we could subsequently laugh at the incident, and continued to talk about our foolishness as we walked towards the end of our farm. After about an hour's hike, we hid among a clump of bushes near the mango tree at the edge of our farm and waited. Behind the mango tree was a large expanse of swamp. Few people ventured there, because it was believed that it was the habitat of camoudies[8] and alligators.

It was getting dark, and without articulating it, we both thought that we were waiting in vain, when we saw a lone Muscovy duck flying towards the tree. It circled two times, as if it was trying to make up its mind, and then landed on one of the top branches. Although

---

[8] South American snake

it was partially covered by the branches, we could see its outline quite clearly. Abel carefully cocked the shotgun, rested it on the branch of small tree so that it would be steady, and took aim. He took pride that he was a good shot, and I had as much, if not more, confidence in him as he had in himself.

We were both aware of the mechanics of the shotgun. When you cock the hammer, a mechanism pulls the firing pin back. Then when you pull the trigger, the pin is propelled forward with force, and strikes the detonator of the cartridge. If you have a bird shot cartridge, many small lead-pellets will be guided through the barrel of the gun, and the pellets will hit the target. If the target is a duck on a tree, the law of gravity dictates that the duck will fall to the ground.

There was a loud boom as Abel pulled the trigger, and I expected to see the duck fall to the ground, but I was disappointed to see it flying away, apparently unharmed.

"Let's go and look under the tree for it," Abel said.

"But I saw it fly away," I told him. "You must have barely missed it," I added, consolingly.

"That must be another duck," Abel stated emphatically. "I don't miss. It has to be under the tree."

He walked purposely towards the mango tree, and I reluctantly followed him, thinking, When he doesn't find the duck, he will accept the fact that he missed.

We searched for half an hour, and of course there was no duck to be found. It was getting quite dark, and even darker under the mango tree, when I gently put my hand on Abel's shoulder. "The duck flew away, Abel. It was on one of the top branches of the tree, and it was a difficult shot. We will try again next weekend."

"It has to be under the tree," Abel insisted. "I rested the gun of a small branch, so the gun wouldn't shake. I'm sure I hit it," he emphasized, as he continued searching under the tree.

When it became so dark that it was impossible to continue searching, we decided to return home along the path we had walked many times before, so the lack of visibility was not a problem.

"We will have better luck next time," I consoled Abel.

Abel still had the determined look on his face as he told me in a confident voice, "We will bring Rex and Brutus, tomorrow morning to search for it. It can't hide from the dogs."

13 PARKING BY THE ROYAL by Ram Jagessar

My schoolteacher buddy, Lallchand, he of the fat belly Indian and shiny head variety, used to live by the Royal Bank in St Augustine, but always told me don't park by the Royal Bank! Not if you are tired of life! That was his little not so *punny* joke if you get my meaning.

"You will get tired of driving if you park your Ford daily by the Royal," he elucidated to me one day, expatiated if you prefer the Trinidad lingo of the time.

"How so?" I said.

"They thieving wind by the bank. And I don't mean the tellers and bean counters inside. Is the tire-jackers in the parking lot. I hear the specialist is a little nasty feller who will take off all four of your tires in less than three minutes. No jack, no helpers, only a little tire iron!" was his replication.

"Impossible! No human being can do that!"

"Pull out your Timex stopwatch and do the countdown. Tire iron at the ready at tire. One jump on the iron at each lug nut to break it and take off the nut in seven seconds. Thirty-five seconds for each tire on a slow day. Two seconds to move to the next tire. All lug nuts off, job done. One hundred and seventy-eight seconds—two minutes 38 seconds!" This in total triumph.

"But the tires still on the car!"

Lallchand shook his head at my ignorance. "Did I say we had twenty-two seconds to spare?"

My face spelled out the impossibility of one man removing four tires in twenty-two seconds. Lallchand looked down at me pitifully.

"No *problemo*. I have complete files. Car is sitting there quiet resting on the bolts going through the rims. Young fellow gives the car a hard push away from him. It moves a few inches, the bolts on the other side go right through the rim until they jam, nothing happens to those two tires. Then right away he pulls the car body back to him hard, bolts on them tires come back clean out of the rim to rest on air, two tires fall flat on the far side, bingo!"

"But that's only two tires!"

"Exercise some patience, boy. The two tires on this side don't fall as the bolts go right through the rim and can go no further. But the bolts on the far side are resting on nothing and that side of the car starts to fall. So mister man gives this side of the car a second hard push as it going down. Bolts come clean out of this side tire rims and this side tires fall *badam* that side, and tires fall *boodoops*, and car drops *bladap* on the hubs."

"I don't believe it!" I exclaimed.

"That is why you fail, young Skywalker!" Lallchand smirked triumphantly.

"Yoda man." I had to concede. "No more Royal parking for me."

14 NANA AND THE DOUGLA GITA by Roop Misir

For at least three times every year, my sister, Bettie, and I would go to the home of Ma's family in Kingston, Leguan Island, Essequibo. Next door lived *Nanee's*[9] elder brother, Parampreet Singh—our *Nana.*[10] As young children, we couldn't pronounce his long first name, but since he lived next door—over there—to me and everyone else, he was known simply as *Ovadeh Nana.*

Ovadeh Nana loved to have his favorite beverage daily just before lunch. So, every day, he would send me to the village rum shop to pick up his Cutdown of Old Grog rum—a small bottle, called a *Flatty* or a *Mickey*, as they would say in Canada. I would put the precious potent potable cargo into a small canvas carrying bag, slung over my growing shoulder. It resembled the one I used to carry my books to school, so no one would suspect what I was secretly carrying.

The rum shop was owned by the village Pandit[11]. However, the licensed shop owner was Shanti—Pandit Shaan's wife. So even though at times Pandit would dispense the potent potable, he was in no way the *official* owner of this popular watering hole.

Nana's drinking problem continued for many years. From one mickey at lunch, he would later order an additional one just before dinner time in the evening.

When I returned for my next annual summer school vacation, Nana would send me three or four times a day for mickies. And in due course, I was getting a bit tired that my holidays were spent with Nana and getting his daily shots of rum. On returning home to Windsor Forest late that August, I told Ma. She promptly alerted Pa

---

[9] Grandmother from mother's side.

[10] Grandfather from mother's side.

[11] Pandits were not supposed to drink alcohol or encourage imbibing.

about Nana and his drinking problem.

Whereupon Pa said, "Look, next time you go to Leguan, I will come with you. And with some luck, I can give Nana some sage advice."

"What do you mean, Pa?" I asked politely.

"He should stop this drinking."

"How Pa?"

"Just do what I do whenever I want to break a bad habit. You remember what I always do when I feel I want to quit smoking?"

"Oh Yes! You would swear and promise, using the *Holy Ramayana*.[12]"

Then one day, Nana paid us a surprise visit to Windsor Forest. He wanted to catch the next train to connect with the Parika ferry to return home to Leguan. However, Ma insisted that he stay over and spend the night. In this way, Pa could meet with Nana and get him to kick the drinking habit. However, Pa came a bit late, just as Nana had finished off a flatty.

I fell asleep but was awakened by a loud discussion between Pa and Nana. Pa told Nana that the secret to good health and happiness was to stop drinking. One or two was okay, but better still was to stop drinking altogether.

"How do you do that, my son?"

"I can tell you what works for me," Pa replied. "It works every time. I used to be a chain smoker, but the doctor warned me to stop, or my lungs would be ruined. The only way I could stop was to swear on the Ramayana."

"Does it work?"

"Oh yes, not only that. I can start back any time I want. and stop again when I have to."

---

[12] The Ramayana is an all-popular epic in Asia. It is the story of King Rama who must save his kidnapped wife, Sita.

Then Nana said, "I prefer the Gita[13]. If you have a copy, bring it and give it to me so I can swear by it?"

From the bookcase, Pa brought a copy of the Bhagavad Gita, with an English translation by Annie Besant.

Nana polished off the last drink from the flattie, and swore with these words, "I swear by this holy book. After this, no more rum for me." From his body language, I sensed Nana wanted to add, *Until the next time.*

However, before he could continue, Ma told him, "I'm so happy for you."

Both Pa and Ma were delighted and congratulated Nana for the courage to take the oath, but I felt remorseful because Nana would no longer give me the usual big jill[14] every day when I had to pick up the flattie of rum from Shaan Maraj rum shop.

Then he reassured me: "Not to worry. Babu. You will still be favorite grandson. Whenever I get change, I always give you money."

During the next Christmas holidays when we visited the extended family at Leguan, I asked where was Nana?

"He is drunk and lying in the hammock at Shankar Mamoo's bottom house," said Budso. "We'll see him when he wakes up."

The next day, when Pa confronted Nana and asked him why he didn't keep his promises, Ovadeh Nana said he had stayed away from drinks for over three months

Finally, one day as Pandit was walking along the village public road, he saw Nana cutting grass for the cows and stopped to greet his former customer.

"Since you returned from Windsor Forest, you never visited our shop. Why are you staying away? Pandit ah na bite people, man!"

---

[13] The Bhagavad Gita is one of the most revered Hindu scriptures.
[14] Coin in Colonial British Guiana; the equivalent of two cents.

"I stopped drinking!"

"You, stopped? What? Drinking? Impossible!"

"Yes, I gave my word on the Gita!"

"Which Gita did you swear on? If you have it, show it to me."

Nana showed the pandit the English translation of the Gita, which he kept in his back pocket. Normally, Pandits are supposed to help their congregation to live by high moral standards—perform worship services, pujas[15], ceremonies, and rituals, not encourage devotees to consume alcohol. However, in this unusual case, Pandit was more of a businessman with an agenda. He would send messages every day, asking Nana to come and visit the shop.

Pandit looked at the translated Gita and turned to Nana. "Ovadeh Nana, this is not the real Gita. It has an English translation. It's a Dougla[16] Gita! The real Gita is written in Sanskrit and Hindi only. No English."

Suddenly, Nana's eyes brightened. He realized that he could have his drinks openly. He was especially happy because Christmas was only a month away.

Pandit Shaan then declared, "When you come to the next time, the drinks will be waiting for you. Welcome back drinks. They will be free, on the house!"

---

[15] A form of ritual prayer and of showing reverence to the Gods.

[16] Person of mixed heritage, mostly Indian and Black.

15 JOHN, RUBY AND SHAKESPEARE by Kennard Ramphal

In 1961, *Twelfth Night*, was required reading for English Language and Literature in the General Certificate of Education, Ordinary Level[17]. It was the first Shakespearean play I read, and I remember it for several reasons.

We lived in colonial British Guiana and my eldest brother, John, who liked to display his knowledge of English to flatter the young women, collaborated with me in reading and interpreting this beautiful Shakespearean comedy.

My eldest brother was very enamoured of the English, and wanted to emulate them as much as our circumstances would allow. With this in mind, he endeavoured to stay out of the sun for lengthy periods, and experimented with various skin-lightening creams and ointments, but was finally resigned to the fact that there was nothing he could do about his color. Having failed to meet an important criterion of being English, John decided to meet the other criteria, within the limitations of the culture of our village.

One of the few ways he did this was by having afternoon tea. Every afternoon at about four, we took a break from our studies and went downstairs to the kitchen, where one of my mother's young sewing apprentices made tea for us. The only treat for us with our tea was the equivalent of a cracker, *salt biscuit*. On this particular day, just before we decided to take our tea, we had been reading *Twelfth Night*, and John was completely obsessed with Shakespeare's mastery of the English language.

"Man, I wish I could write like him," he told Abel and me. "There is no other writer in greater command of the English language than Shakespeare. Look at how Viola sweet-talked Olivia!

---

[17] Grade 12 equivalent in North America.

I wish that I can flatter a girl like that," he said, as we made our way downstairs.

On this particular afternoon Ruby, who had recently joined the four young women in my mom's sewing class, volunteered to make tea for us. Ruby was a dark, eighteen-year-old with sparkling eyes and long hair, falling loosely down her back. Her prominent breasts were supported by a brassiere-front dress, a special dress made to accommodate the breasts, because very few women in the village wore brassieres, which had to be purchased in Georgetown, and were expensive. Like most girls in our village, Ruby wore no make-up. Villagers made fun of the few women who put on make-up, and one woman who had recently married and moved to the village, had applied some Ponds powder on her face when she went to pick coffee beans. She was called *Ponds Powder* by everybody in the village for the rest of her life.

Ruby was the eldest child in her family, and her parents had pulled her out of school as soon as she was old enough to look after her two siblings. Her mother, who worked in the Weeding Gang[18] in Wales Sugar Estate, had taught her to cook as soon as she was tall enough to reach the fireside, and all that remained in her preparation for marriage was for her to learn to sew. At the time the incidents related in this story occurred, that aspect of her learning was being addressed.

John got the crackers from my parents' small grocery store, and put them on a plate with some *Cow and Girl* butter, as Ruby heated the water for tea. It was a warm day, and the heat from the wood fireplace caused Ruby to perspire, as she put some tea leaves in the water boiling on the fireside. She allowed the brew to steep for a few minutes before straining, then she added condensed milk and sugar, and poured the tea in three enamel cups. Ruby smiled seductively at John as she placed two cups on the table, before returning to the small stand beside the fireside to bring the third.

John's mind was working overtime as he searched for the appropriate language to impress the dark-skinned beauty. Then he

---

[18] The group of people hired to get rid of weeds around the plantation.

remembered *Twelfth Night*. As Ruby—face damp with sweat, put the third cup on the table, John looked lovingly at her.

"'Tis beauty truly blent," he said in his best imitation of an *English accent*. With his hand stretched towards Ruby, he continued, "whose red and white nature's own sweet and cunning hand laid on. Lady, you are the cruel'st she alive/If you will lead these graces to the grave/And leave the world no copy."

Ruby froze like a deer caught in the headlights of a car, and looked at John in bewilderment. I could almost hear her brain torturing itself as it tried in vain to make sense of what she heard. She knew that it was not Creole, and was fairly certain that it was not Standard English, because she had listened to our radio many times, and most of the programs were in English.

When she finally realized that she could not figure out what John was saying, and what language he was speaking, she gave vent to her frustration. "Talk English you rass,[19]" she exhorted, as she exited the kitchen and joined the other trainees in the sewing area.

---

[19] Local swear word

16 WINNING WITHOUT FIGHTING by Ram Jagessar

Once in Trinidad as a young university graduate, I went into a bar in Curepe, ordered a cold beer and sat at the counter drinking it.

In less than a minute a young Black fellow came up on my left and snarled belligerently, "Hey you, Indian!"

I turned to my left, looked at him, saw nothing there to merit my attention, and returned to my beer.

The young man, now about five feet away from me, continued, "You think you smart? You think you better than me?"

I ignored him completely, even though he was only five feet away. But I kept a look at him from the corner of my eye, as my sensei had advised. He could hit me suddenly, but he would have to make a step forward to do it and I would be ready.

He continued in the same vein for a couple more taunts while I showed no response at all. *I was saying to myself,* This dummy is just looking for blows. He's threatening a purple belt karateka with a full bottle of beer in his hand. If he only makes a move towards me, I will have to smash his face with this bottle.

My silence and inattention were apparently not what the Black youth expected in that now dead quiet bar, and shortly he turned away and disappeared into the back of the bar. I finished my beer and left. The bar resumed its usual activity and conversation.

Obviously, the others in the bar knew what was going on, but were not prepared to intervene. The young fellow would pick an easy target like a slightly built young Indian with thick glasses and scare the target into buying him a drink or giving him some money. It hadn't worked, thanks to the Trinidad Karate Association at the university.

The first group I joined was the Karate Club at the university of the West Indies, St Augustine, Trinidad, a branch of the Trinidad Karate Association. It was 1967 and I was 19, in my first year and my first semester at the university, and in the prime of my life. That group has been a grand blessing, helping enormously to make me the fearless iconoclast I hope I've been in my life. No man can intimidate me. No man has intimidated me in the last 50 odd years since I joined that karate club, and yet I haven't been in any fist fight or street fight, nor needed to use those karate self-defence skills.

I've joined five other martial arts groups in Trinidad and Canada since those university days, and the message has been the same. If you learned to defend yourself from physical attack you probably won't need to defend yourself. By your bearing and the way you respond to a threatened attack, you silently project the air of a person who can hold his own, who will not be an easy target. The bullies, who usually start street fights. will pass you up and look for a person who will project fear and weakness.

Another occasion, this time in Toronto about four years ago, I was doing my seniors mall-walk alone at the Cedarbrae Mall without incident as usual. Just another frail looking seventy-year-old Indian man getting some exercise. I walked past a group of four teen boys, one Black and three White kids probably no more than fifteen years old, moving in the opposite direction. Nothing to do with me. Then the whole group turned and ran back behind me and I saw the Black kid run up and block my path forward. I stopped, but said nothing.

Black kid said sternly, "You burped in my face!"

I said nothing but looked at him quizzically within an arm's length of me.

"You burped in my face!" This time more threateningly.

It just came out of me without thinking—the response of a karate black belt. "You want to make something out of it?" My response was accompanied by a hard stare into his hungry eyes.

He was startled and almost physically recoiled, obviously not expecting this from an old geezer. I moved around him and resumed my walk. I never saw that group of kids in the mall again.

Later I realized what had happened. The gang, obviously without any money, thought they would troll the mall looking for some easily frightened old fogey, find a reason to confront said fogey, scare the pants off him, get a donation of some cash and head for the game room or the food court. But they were young in the game and had misread the target.

All I could say was, "Thank you Sensei Number 1, Sensei Number 2. Thanks to all my sanseis, including Sensei Harry Persaud who awarded me my black belt after nine years of training."

They all had the same message: the best fight is when you win without fighting.

17 CHACHEE'S BABIES by Roop Misir

In our custom, traditionally, married couples like to have children and start their families early. However, in his two previous marriages, my Chacha[20] sired no offspring. Not unexpectedly, the unions ended in marriage breakdown and separation. So, for the third time, he decided to remarry and hoped to have a baby, even though my new Chachee[21] came with her five-year-old son from a previous marriage.

For the first few years, the family lived a happy life, except that Chachee showed no signs of getting pregnant. Repeated attempts to conceive ended in miscarriages or stillbirths. Unhappy with the doctors, they decided to try the non-medical, more traditional approaches to conception.

Although Chacha and Chachee were Hindus, they felt so desperate for a new baby that they sought the help of holy men from all faiths. Naturally, they consulted Pandits[22], as well as Majees[23] and Christian priests. The belief is that since the divine is the driving force to make even the most improbable event or wish to happen, help from any and every source would make them achieve their objective. God is God. God is Great—regardless.

The couple listened to the holy men, but the one that impressed them most was Akbar, the village Majee. After the first session, Majee discussed the implications of invoking Allah Almighty to end the baby drought. In the event of a successful birth, the Majee would arrange for a Muslim couple, already with children of their own, to be designated as the new parent-guardian. As an act of good faith, the couple would give Chacha and Chachee the payment of one

---

[20] Hindi: Father's brother
[21] Wife of my father's brother
[22] Hindu Priests
[23] Muslim Cleric

shilling[24,] supposedly the token price of the baby. Henceforth, the Muslim couple, Narima and Shaheed, would also be the de-facto parents.

Then Majee stipulated, "You must offer daily Namaz[25] and pray to Allah. The Almighty bestows blessings on the faithful. It's quite possible that your lady could conceive successfully and bear a healthy baby to term. Do remember, Faith and sincerity are vital to success. Allahu Akbar!"

Majee advised that this approach was not without payback. If Chachee gave birth to a full-term bouncing baby, one of Majee expectations would be for Chacha, Chachee, and the family to convert to Islam, or at least follow the Islamic tradition. This dilemma worried Chacha quite a bit because nothing in the whole wide world would get him to jump the ship of religion—from a practicing Hindu to a staunch *Mussalman*. As a high-caste Hindu Brahmin, Chacha felt uncomfortable. Still, he was determined to get the little bundle of joy. Regardless, some good could come out of the entire exercise. So, for the time being, he nodded.

There must be a way this situation could be avoided, he thought. Chacha was well-known for his great respect for others and their belief systems. To his mind, all religions led to the same goal. Much like all rivers ultimately flowing into the large ocean. He soliloquized that what the world needed was desirable universal traits—humility, kindness, and acts of humanity, not petty differences that tended to divide the human family. He thought: In our tradition, the world is one family[26]. Therefore, if there is one God, don't other religions adore other manifestations of the same God?

As it turned out nine months later, Chachee gave birth to a full-term bouncing baby boy! As per the oral understanding, the boy was presented to the adopted parents, Narima and Shaheed, who gave him the Muslim name, Tarek, which meant Morning Star.

Little Tarek spent time with his adopted parents on Muslim special days, enabling him to get acquainted with the Islamic culture

---

[24] Twenty-four cents Sterling
[25] Muslim prayers.
[26] *Sanskrit: Vasudeva Kutumbakam.*

and traditional way of life. He also visited the Madrassa[27] and attended the *Masjid*[28]. In practice, however, it was expedient for the two families to live closely—more like an extended family than to follow the expected religious routines to the letter. The common thread linking both families was that their ancestors were originally from India. This factor, more than any other, helped to mitigate the rigidity required of new converts to Islam.

In subsequent years, Chachee gave birth to two more babies—a girl and a boy. With the adopted family having five children of their own, and Chacha and Chachee with four, the two families had a combined total of nine children, altogether a family membership of thirteen.

In the real world, there's a need for tolerance and respect for other peoples' religions, cultures, and freedom of thought. Cognizant of these, both families would turn out in full force at family events—social, cultural, and religious. And whether the Divine was Ram[29] or Raheem[30],they would offer praise to God, chanting: *Ishwar Allah tero naam.*[31]

As it turned out, Chacha got his wish. The families learned from each other and chose the unorthodox but practical way to live.

Majee was surprised to learn that the ancestors of both couples were Hindus. In a world where Hindus and Muslims intermingled, mixed, and lived side by side, he also recognized the current dynamic world of change. Also, their entire village community was a vibrant multifaith, multicultural milieu.

So, what to do? The lyrics of the Hindi song (sung by Pradeep) echoes it all:

"Kitna Badal Gaya Insaan! (कितना बदल गया इंसान!)"

How much man has changed!

---

[27] School for Islamic instruction
[28] Ararbic word for Mosque.
[29] Hindu God.
[30] Compassionate or merciful in Islam
[31] Your name is Ishwar; your name is Allah.

18 THE MORNING I PLAYED DEAD by Kennard Ramphal

"I told you not to cut grass from Balgobin land," my father scolded me, as his leather belt met my twelve-year-old bottom on a sunny Friday afternoon. His face was flushed with alcohol and anger.

One of my chores every afternoon was to cut a bundle of grass for our black and white cow. We could not allow the cow to roam free, because of the danger of it going into one of our neighbors' properties and destroying their vegetable gardens or the cassava and plantain plants in their farm. The bundle of grass every afternoon was to ensure that it got enough to eat when I brought it in its pen for the night. I had cut the lush grass from Balgobin's land, after repeated warnings from my father not to do so.

Balgobin does not have a cow, or sheep, or goats, I had rationalized. Why can't I cut grass from his land? The grass is tall and green, and I can cut a bundle very quickly.

After I was punished, I acknowledged the fact that I should not have ventured on Balgobin's land, but I felt that I did not deserve the pain and the humiliation inflicted on me by my father. I convinced myself that I was a good son. Every morning, my job was to take the cow out of the pen, and tether it in a spot where there was enough grass for it to graze on. Then I cleaned the pen, and threw the dung in a heap where it composted before it was used as manure for our small, but lush vegetable garden. I then watered the lettuce, bora, boulangers and other plants in the garden, using water from the rain barrel by the side of the house, Then I showered, ate breakfast, and headed out to school on schooldays, where I was considered an excellent student, who almost always placed first in class. I brooded the entire summer holidays, when Ramesh Mangal, who was a close friend of mine, beat me by two marks and placed first, relegating me to second place.

I knew my parents loved me, and it puzzled me that my father had punished me so brutally for what I considered a minor infraction. He had just come home from Manbahal's rum shop and grocery store, staggering slightly, when Balgobin accosted him as he turned into our yard. Balgobin lived two house lots away, and apparently sat on his front steps and waited for my father to come home. He was wearing a dirty khaki trousers, and a T-shirt whose color could not be determined because of the layers of dust and mud. An old, floppy Wilson hat, ventilated with moth-created holes, graced his head. The entire village of Canal Number 2 was aware that Balgobin always wore this hat because he was quite bald, although he was still in his forties. When he first started wearing the hat, his acquaintances would playfully take off his hat when they greeted him, allowing anyone who was nearby to see the reflection of the sun on his shining bald head. Frustrated and humiliated, he let it be known that he would slap anybody who dared to take off his hat in future. This threat successfully restrained his friends, and his hat remained on his head.

"I tell you to tell your son not to cut grass from my land," he had told my father. "The long grass full his eye[32] and he cut the grass I been saving for Balram. You know that he is my wife's cousin, and they give me milk every morning. I tell them that I gon keep the grass for them to cut. You want to keep cow, grow your own grass," he admonished my father as he turned to go home, leaving my father angry and speechless.

My backside felt the pain of my father's encounter with Balgobin, as I went to sleep on my tummy, and plotted how to retaliate for being unjustly punished. Sometime in the night, between sleep and wake, the answer came to me. I will play dead. That would teach my father a lesson.

In the morning, I did not get up with my two brothers, but remained in bed, slowed down my breathing, and wondered how long it would take my family to miss me. I wanted to pee, but not so badly that it made me think of abandoning my plan. To my surprise, I could hear everybody in the household going about his or her tasks

---

[32] Made him greedy.

as if everything was normal. My mom was cooking in the kitchen, my father was puttering in the yard, and I could hear my two brothers gargling as they brushed their teeth and rinsed their mouth. If I play dead long enough, they have to notice, I thought, even as my bladder expanded to uncontrollable proportions.

I lay still and took shallow breaths, so that my abdomen did not rise and fall with my breathing, hoping that someone would look in and see me in the death posture. The minutes passed slowly.

I heard my eldest brother, Kumar shout, "Ma, pass another roti."

"And give me some more bora," Jai, my other brother requested. By then, my thighs felt damp, and my stomach was rumbling. "Ma, you better give me some roti too," Jai told my mother.

I wondered if they were doing this for my benefit! Did they know what I was up to? I knew that I could bear the hunger for a while longer, but my expanding bladder was weakening my resolve. By then, there were more than just a few drops of liquid on my thighs, and I clenched my teeth as I endeavored to stop the flow of liquid. When I heard the sound of the water running as my mother washed the dishes in the sink, I could wait no longer.

I grimaced as I got up, rushed out of the bedroom and out the back door, leaned against the nearest orange tree, and relieved my grateful bladder. My father, who was mending the gate of the garden fence, came up to me.

"Balgobin insult me yesterday. That's why I was angry with you," my father said by way of an apology. "Your mom cook roti and bora. Go and eat. But wash your hands first," he added as he looked down at my hands buttoning my fly.

My mom had already dished out my food when I entered the kitchen, after washing my hands at the barrel. It seemed as if everybody's eyes were on me, as I ate like a person who had come back from the dead.

19 A WILD MAN SAVED MY CAREER by Ram Jagessar

When the final exams for my B.A. at the University of the West Indies came around, I knew I was going to fail.

Friends and family believed implicitly, without any evidence, that I was going to shine. But I knew that I hadn't done one tenth of the studies that the other students had done in the last two years. And yes! They were the same exciting two years before the 1970 insurrection[33] and state of emergency. Who could study in such a time?

They say when you need him most, a guru appears. Mine took the form of a genial, balding English lecturer named Warren. He was a very unconventional lecturer by any count. A few weeks before final exams, Warren told my English Literature class that he couldn't give us any tip about the actual questions. But he could tell us how to do well in all the exams with a kind of unconventional guerilla strategy. I don't think anybody listened but me.

He counselled us to look at the final exams from the point of view of the person like him grading the papers. His advice was to be bold, be creative, be sneaky, be irrelevant even, but never be dull and pedantic. Be your best as a writer and give the lecturer reading the papers something interesting and different.

Now what kind of lunatic lecturer will tell undergraduates to be daring and creative, and even irrelevant in their final exams? That was Warren, a wild man by any count.

What kind of idiot student will take such a chance with an exam that will determine his work career, his life? That would be me, destined to fail, desperate for a *Hail Mary* pass to score a touchdown.

---

[33] The Black Power movement in Trinidad exploded as thousands took to the streets in demonstrations. The government arrested activists and declared a State Of Emergency.

Naturally, everybody ignored this crazy *limey* but me.

I was way behind in studies, and had missed many classes. In fact, I had done no work at all in my second year, and precious little in my third and final year. I found myself two months before finals, a full year and three quarters behind my classmates. No way could I catch up with those who had studied hard for two years, had mountains of notes, and had read all the reference books in the library.

Warren had advised us to take a risk, and avoid the topics that most of the class would be answering, because to get top marks you have to be better than all of them, and that ain't easy since most of them have done their homework.

Pick a less popular topic that is on the syllabus, and always anticipate a question on the final examination, but for which there may not even have been a single lecture. If you are the only person, or one of the handful answering that topic, it's hard for the examiner to compare your effort with other classmates, and he has to give you high marks. Plus, if you make errors, he may not spot them because he hadn't read up or lectured on that topic for many years. An additional bonus is that he's glad to see something different from yet another boring pedantic answer on the popular topic, and you already have five or ten marks for being different.

This was how I worked it.

In English literature we studied the Romantic poets and 19th century Victorians with people like Wordsworth, Keats, Byron, Shelley and the like. When the final exam came, most people but me chose to answer questions on those folks who had been lectured upon and studied in fine detail.

I chose to focus on Thomas Love Peacock who had written five little novels, but on whom there had been no lecture at all. I read his five little novels and the single book of literary criticism in the library. You know how many books there are on writers like Shelley and Keats? My fellow students had read them all. I had read none.

When the exam came sure enough there was one question on

Peacock and I killed it. Pretty sure nobody else in U.W.I.[34] had answered that topic, so if I made mistakes in my answer the examiner wouldn't be sure. Would he go and read up the five novels just to check my answer? No way!

But in evaluating the answers on Keats, most students would have the facts right, and if anyone got something wrong or forgot to put in something important, said examiner would know instantly. Plus, each answer on Keats would be judged in comparison to the best answers, and the person would have to come good to get the higher marks. On the contrary, my answer on Peacock would stand alone like the *Colossus of Rhodes*.

Lecturer Warren said it was terribly boring and painful to grade 50 student answers on Keats, all of them saying essentially the same thing and plodding along like steamrollers. Any answer that was different, that was lively, that was entertaining, that was a pleasure to read, even if some of it was irrelevant, was like a tonic to a tired lecturer.

I thought, *Warren Baba*, you preached and I answered. I wrote my best work in those exams, dancing the light fantastic like nobody else would have dared to do. I used the same strategy in my other English and History classes, and told no one, not even my girlfriend at the time. She was quite conservative and cautious, and would have been horrified.

The final results showed that Warren was dead right.

I believe I was the only one to get an Upper-Second-Class honours and should have gotten First Class Honours but for a mean old wretch, Dr Millette, who marked extra hard so that nobody could get higher class degrees and go on to get a Masters and a Ph.D. to compete with him. The university fired him some years later. Most people in my classes got bare passes for their B.A., and just a few got Lower Seconds.

But I didn't care.

I had gotten the big one, the springboard to later success. My university colleagues never understood why I had scored big—they

---

[34] University of the West Indies

knew I hadn't studied hard like they did, and had missed so many classes. I didn't tell them my Warren secret. They wouldn't have dared to use it anyway. But me, I was desperate, I would have tried anything that was legal.

And, *Yessir!* The U.W.I. degree and the Warren unconventional approach got me into teaching, into journalism and public relations, which turned out to be the skills that got me a resident visa to Canada and to escape from Trinidad.

So, what can I say? A trillion cheers for lecturer Warren, who probably passed away by now. I will always treasure his memory.

20 A SLEEPY CANE HAULER MISADVENTURE by Roop Misir

Farming has always been a challenging occupation for people in the rural areas. of Guyana. In the early 1960s., much of this was done on the flat alluvial coast, as well as along the hilly sand and clay riverain areas. Along the West Coast and West Bank of the Demerara River, a variety of crops was cultivated. The main crops were sugarcane and rice, and cash crops like ground provisions, coffee, and cocoa along the bank, mainly in Canal Number One and Two Polders[35].

Life in British Guiana was hard and laborious, and people wanted change. And yes, freedom did come, but at a painful price. Ongoing unrest manifested itself in race riots in the early 1960s.

SWEET SUGAR

Canals No. One and Two were the main suppliers of ground provisions and fresh fruits, notably oranges and pineapples. One consequence of the race riots was that the flow of provisions from Canals One and Two Polders to Georgetown and other parts of the coast was interrupted. Faced with hard times, some farmers started to plant rice; others switched to sugar cane.

Eventually, sugar cane became a successful and highly profitable crop. The cane was cut and then transported by tractor-drawn trailers to nearby estates of Leonora, or Wales. For many years, sweet sugar defined the rural agricultural economy of both Canals One and Two.

Leonora was about five miles west of my village, Windsor Forest. From my house, we could hear vehicles rumbling along the

---

[35] From Dutch: a piece of low-lying land reclaimed from the sea or a river and protected by dikes.

West Coast Public Road. At times, usually at night, I would see trailers, piled high with newly cut cane, being taken for delivery to the Leonora factory.

Often cane haulers would stop at Morgan's Rum Shop for a drink, plus snacks and sardine sandwiches. Since I used to hang out at this watering hole, I got to know most of the cane haulers. One chap, Prakash, used to talk only about cane, and how he would take two or three loads in one night. I got to know him very well.

GOING FOR CANE

One evening, Prakash told me, "Tomorrow, I will come again, and then go for more cane!"

I was not sure whether he meant hauling an additional trailer load of cane, or checking out his sweet girl, Lolita, up on Main Street after a busy night's work. After I had my fill of fun at Morgan's Rum Shop, I staggered home just before midnight and was sound asleep when I was aroused by a loud knocking at my bedroom door. My bedside alarm clock indicated that the time was 2:30 a.m.

I was still halfway between wake and sleep when I heard an insistent voice. "Baboo, Baboo, wake up. Wake up!"

Still groggy, I lay back down, ignoring the knocking and the loud voice, but the knocking continued relentlessly at my door. Opening my eyes, I reluctantly stumbled to the door and opened it.

Prakash, panting for breath, spoke with a trembling voice: "Baboo, I am in trouble."

"Wadiya mean, *trouble*?"

"Yes, Baboo, trouble. Big trouble!?"

"OK, tell me."

"Come, start your motorbike, and let's go now. *Right now!*"

Seeing that my friend was obviously in distress, I grabbed the key for my motorcycle and asked him to sit on the pillion rider seat.

"You have to take me home now. I must get home and go back

to bed before day clean, man."

"Why?"

"I drove my trailer with a big load of cane into the trench by Morgan's Rum Shop. I must reach home under the cover of darkness so that no one will see me around the trailer in the trench."

"So, you did go for cane. Was it your second trailer load?"

He did not answer, but jumped on the seat and held on to me as I raced east along the West Coast to Vreed-en-hoop, then south down the West Bank Road, and west into Canal Number 1 in record time. He thanked me gratefully. and remarked that I saved the day!

"Prakash, I always warn you not to drink and drive. If you must drink and drive, then drink sweet drink or mauby."

I left him to ponder because I had to get home in forty minutes to review my lesson notes. I had a very busy day at school that day.

While driving back home to Windsor Forest. I realized I hadn't taken the time to ask Prakash about details of what happened before he drove the trailer full of cane into the Canal. But I did have my suspicions. I did know that he would haul his cane to Leonora. Also, he would do jobs by transporting cane for other farmers in the district. What baffled me though, was whether this particular load was a contracted job, or whether he hitched his tractor to a trailer full of cane without the farmer's permission. In effect, stealing!

That unusual event happened nearly fifty years ago.

On a trip to Canal Number 1 to visit my Mausi[1], Prakash's neighbor, I asked about Prakash's whereabouts. Mausi said that Prakash knew that I was coming, so he decided to go to buy a bottle of rum for us to drink.

So, I waited and waited and waited. A few hours later, I left Canal Number One, and also Mausi, and Prakash's wife and family.

I never heard from Prakash again.

[1] Auntie (Mother's sister).

21 PERSISTENT JEWARHIRLALL by Kennard Ramphal

My elder brother's first name was Jewarhirlall, but everybody called him Jai. Jai and I were two of the seven students from our school in Canal No. 2 Polder who wrote the Pupil Teachers' Appointment (P.T.A.) examination. Students who were successful in this exam were eligible to become pupil teachers—literally teachers who were learning to teach under the guidance of a more experienced teacher. In the past, the names of successful candidates were published in the daily newspapers, but in the year we wrote the exam, for reasons known only to the officials of the Ministry of Education, letters were sent to the headmasters of the schools in which students were successful, asking them to advise students that they had to attend interviews with an official from the Ministry of Education.

One Tuesday evening, we had just finished dinner, and Jai and I were upstairs at the table studying, while Ma and Daddy were in the kitchen. We were alerted to the presence of a visitor by the barking of Rex and Brutus, our black and white dogs. When Daddy went outside to restrain the dogs and welcome the visitor, he was surprised to see Jack Mungal, whom everybody in the village called *Teacher Jack*. Teacher Jack, a lanky six-footer and the Deputy Headmaster of our school, was in the process of dismounting from his bicycle when Daddy greeted him.

"The dogs just bark; they won't bite," Daddy reassured him.

Teacher Jack did not reply to Daddy's observation, but said, "I got good news for you, Mr. Ramphal." Then he pulled out a letter from the pocket of his shirt and gave it to Daddy as he continued, "Deomitr passed the P.T.A. exam. He has to go for an interview with Mr. Slanger Davies, the headmaster of Queen's College, next week Wednesday at eleven o'clock."

Daddy was quiet for quite some time, before he asked Teacher Jack, "Only Deomitr? What about Jewahirlall? He study hard for the exam, too."

"We got the letter only for Deomitr," Teacher Jack replied, noncommittedly.

Although one of his sons had failed the examination, daddy wanted to show his appreciation to Teacher Jack for taking the trouble of coming to our house and inform us that I passed.

He told Ma, "Give Deomitr some money for him to go to Sedan and buy a bottle of El Dorado." After receiving the money from Ma, I immediately left for Sedan's rum shop, which was conveniently located three houses away, while Ma was endeavoring to console my brother.

"Don't worry, Jai! We gon send you back next year to write the exam. You bright. You gon pass next time."

"I can't fail," my brother insisted. "I gon go to the interview and tell them I passed."

Jai had every reason to feel confident that he had passed the exam. After we completed the exams for the various subjects, we had compared notes. We had arrived at the same answers for arithmetic, and while the answers to the other subjects were not as straightforward, he was certain that he did as well as, if not better, than I.

The following day, when Ma picked up my white shirt to wash, Jai brought his blue shirt to her. As I was polishing my shoes, Jai sat beside me, and started to polish *his* shoes. Later, when Ma was ironing my shirt and trousers, Jai handed her the shirt and trousers he intended to wear. Ma accepted Jai's clothes with a sad and perplexed look, and thought desperately of ways in which she could comfort her son.

On the evening before the interview, Jai was as ready as I was, although Ma and Daddy tried to convince him that Teacher Jack said that only I was to attend an interview. When I hung the clothes I planned to wear on the nail behind the door of our bedroom, Ma and Daddy looked sadly at Jai as he selected the clothes which he intended to wear. The silence was broken by the barking of Rex and Brutus, and when Daddy went downstairs, we heard the familiar voice of Teacher Jack.

"Jewarhirlall also passed the exam." Teacher Jack intentionally spoke loudly so that we could hear him clearly upstairs.

Daddy hushed the dogs, and ushered Teacher Jack upstairs, where Jai and I looked at each other. Jai was smiling and looked at me as if to say, *I told you I passed.*

As soon as he entered the door, Teacher Jack stretched out his hand. "Congratulations Jewarhirlall! You passed!" Then he sat on one of the chairs around the table, and explained to everyone. "The clerks at the Ministry of Education made a mistake, and sent the letter that Jewarhirlall passed to the school in Canal No. 1. Mr. Sahai, the headmaster, sent somebody with your letter to me this afternoon. Jewarhirlall, you have to attend an interview tomorrow. You don't have a lot of time to prepare."

Jai simply said, "Teacher Jack, I know that I passed, and I am prepared."

Ma, who had come upstairs from the kitchen to join us, had the widest smile I ever saw, even though there were tears in her eyes.

Daddy was also smiling, but with more restraint, as he fished a five-dollar bill out of his pocket, handed it to Jai, and instructed him, "Go to Seedan and buy a bottle of rum."

"They got to go to the interview tomorrow," Ma reminded Daddy.

Daddy laughed loudly as he looked at Ma, then at Teacher Jack, and then again at Ma, before he responded, "Jai and Deomitr got interview tomorrow. I don't have no interview. Teacher Jack you have any interview tomorrow?" Teacher Jack recognized it as a rhetorical question and just looked at Daddy and smiled.

Before he left to go to the rum shop, my elder brother looked at

Teacher Jack intensely. "Teacher Jack, I was going to go to the interview and tell them I passed."

Nobody minded when the Daddy and Teacher Jack drank late into the night.

The following day, both Jai and I were successful at the interview, and became pupil teachers, after being baptized and changing our names to *Abel* and *Kennard*.

We did not particularly appreciate the fact that we had to be baptized before being hired as teachers, but I will forever admire my elder bother for his unwavering confidence and his refusal to believe that he failed an examination in which he had done so well.

22 JANKAN WIFE COULDN'T TALK HINDI by Ram Jagessar

Jankan young wife could cook and clean and mind baby, but she couldn't talk Hindi.

All of us in Mora Dam Road were a little surprised when she started saying something like Hindi. The older people, like Jankan father, Papa Sam, say it sounded like Hindi but made no sense, so everybody agree she was catching spirit[36]. They didn't say she gone mad, or was a crazy woman, but catching spirit was something all could understand.

Then when she stopped cooking and cleaning in the tiny one room shack next to my cousin Rajdai house, that she and the two-year-old pickney shared with Jankan, all man jack agree something had to be done. They send for the obeah man, the Spirit doctor. No point going by the regular doctor, by name Dr Macoon, in Penal junction, because pills and injection have no effect on Spirit.

We young teenage boys sit down on a long bench under Rajdai house to see the action. Anybody else who had nothing to do also crowd around to see the Obeah Man arrive to handle the Spirit. Obeah man didn't look like anything special, just a young fellow in pants and blue shirt looking very important with himself.

We point out Jankan wife sitting down quiet on the bed in the shack, facing us with the door open and the board window open with a stick behind the bed. She was very thin and very young, probably not much older that us boys. They marry them early in Mora Dam Road, Penal.

Blue Shirt Obeah Man walk up slowly and very confidently to Jankan wife, saying something very soft that we couldn't hear, like,

---

[36] Possessed

"When you going up to a bad dog to put the dog chain on him?"

Jankan wife ain't say nothing, never move. Blue Shirt now by the open door gone in the shack, and make two step towards Jankan wife with his hands in front of him. We couldn't see if he had anything in his hands, as his back was blocking the view. Blue Shirt make another step and now he almost reach Jankan wife sitting motionless on the bed. It was a small shack and the bed took up most of the space.

Before he could make another step, Jankan wife launched off the bed at him, snarling like the woman vampire in *Bride of Dracula*. She was looking to bite him in the face or neck. Her hands and fingernails open up to claw the obeah man. On the bench we young boys jumped. Obeah Man jumped too. He ducked to one side to escape Jankan wife, and dived over the bed and out the open window like a Hollywood stunt man.

Last we saw of him he was running down the hill and away. Jankan wife sit back down on the bed real quiet, face calm like a preacher man.

The watching crowd buzzed like a disturbed *Jack Spaniard* nest at this exciting development. Runners went out to the village to carry the news that the obeah man had failed. We young boys refused to move from our bench, as the talk was they were sending for another obeah man with more *ju ju*.

About two hours later we see a taxi pull up and out comes obeah man number two. He didn't look like anything special either, pants and shirt and a little handbag, a middle-aged man with plenty gray hair. He had the board-window closed. Then he walked in the shack and closed the door behind him. We boys on the bench groaned. We wouldn't see any of the action.

In a really short time, no more than two minutes, the door opened and obeah man, number two, came out the shack with a lock of Jankan wife black hair in his hands. He took out a long six-inch spike from his bag and wrapped the hair around it and walked towards the mango tree by the side of Rajdai house. We all trooped behind him.

At the mango tree, Obeah Man pulled out a hammer from his handbag and hammered the spike and hair into the thick mango tree trunk, right up to the head. Then he turned and walked away without another word.

Jankan wife stopped talking Hindi on the spot. She went back to cleaning and cooking and washing child diaper as if nothing happen.

We young boys tried to pull out the spike with the hair, but we couldn't. It had gone in the full six inches. It probably still in the mango tree today.

I wonder if somebody pull it out today, will Jankan wife start talking Hindi again?

23 RAMLALL'S STRANGE COURTSHIP by Kennard Ramphal

My uncle, Ramlall, lived about a mile west of where we lived in the village of Canal No. 2, and his courtship and upcoming wedding were much talked about in the village.

Ramlall, about five feet, ten inches tall, his hair, shiny with coconut oil, combed straight back with a part on the left side, was twenty-three years old, and was a smart, handsome guy. He was one of the few people in Canal who attended high school in Georgetown, the capital of Guyana, about twelve miles away from our residence. My uncle was pulled out of Wray High School after only three weeks, because he was offered a coveted job in the factory at Wales Estate. However, he shared a phrase with us, which according to him, was French. For months, we walked around the village, saying, "La cuisiniere la repas is le la cuisine," proud that we could speak French. I learned later that there is no French phrase like that, but that is another story.

My uncle was responsible for ensuring that the temperature of the cane juice being boiled to make the sugar remained constant. Consequently, he was always neatly dressed, with a sharp crease in his trousers, his shirt carefully starched and pressed, and his shoes polished to a shine. He rode his new Humber bicycle with a swagger to work every day because the estate truck, which transported workers to the sugar estate and back to our village, did not offer him the flexibility he desired. In addition, he did not want to mix with the workers who cut cane or were in the weeding-gang, whom he considered lower than himself.

Midway between the sugar factory and his home lived the object of his desires, a buxom girl named Sunita whose prominent breasts were accentuated by the tight blouse which was always a part of her outfit. She wore her hair in a ponytail, flipped over her shoulder and resting between her breasts.

Sunita waited every day, in her bottom-house[37] to get a glimpse of Ramlall, or for him to get a glimpse of her, and her breasts. Often, Ramlall showed off by taking both hands off the handle of the bicycle, and wave to her. For weeks, my uncle racked his brains in vain to find an excuse to stop and talk with Sunita. He had almost given up trying, when his bowels provided the solution just as he approached her home.

Sunita expected him to glance at her, as he always did, raise his hand, and ride on. Instead, he steered his bicycle towards her house, crossed the plank which served as a bridge across the four-foot-deep drain, and rode straight to the bottom-house.

"Where you all latrine?" he said. "A strong shit hold me."

"The latrine deh fifty yards behind, along this path. Follow yuh nose," she added with a smile, as she gave him a page of *The Daily Chronicle*[38] to be used as toilet paper.

Ramlall leaned his bicycle against one of the posts of the house, and hurried along the path, the single page of *The Daily Chronicle* clasped in his hand, while Sunita waited for his return. Her parents had not yet returned from the farm, and did not know of the attraction between her and Ramlall. If they come home, I will explain that he just come in to use our latrine, she rationalized. This thought relaxed her, and she was excited because of Ramlall's nearness. She thought, He, too, never see me so close, and was glad that she had combed her hair, and had put some *Ponds* powder on her face earlier that day.

When she saw Ramlall walking along the path between the coffee trees, he was looking much more relaxed. He had recently seen the film, *High School Confidential*, and was attempting to affect a swagger he had admired in Russ Tamblyn, lamenting the fact that he did not have a sweater to throw over his shoulder. When Sunita pulled on her ponytail, causing her tight blouse to allow her breasts to be even more prominent, Ramlall stopped walking, mesmerized.

---

[37] Houses were built on posts with the bottom open out and referred to as the Bottom-house.

[38] One of the two daily newspapers in the country; the other was the Guiana Graphic.

As he approached the bottom house, and went to the standpipe to wash his hands, he felt that he couldn't just jump on his bicycle and ride away, but had to say something to Sunita.

"You all latrine really stink," he observed.

Quick as a flash came her reply. "Na shit! It na must stink!"

Ramlall was impressed by her wit, but couldn't come up with an excuse to linger any longer. However, he was satisfied that he had found a reason to talk to his beloved. The next afternoon, Sunita was not surprised to see him ride his bicycle under the bottom-house again. The truth was that Ramlall wanted to go to the toilet after his shift finished at the factory, but decided to wait until he reached Sunita's house. She was half expecting him to stop, and had a sheet of *The Chronicle* ready for him. Ramlall walked more leisurely than he did the previous day, and decided to forego the swagger of Russ Tamblyn.

As he returned from the latrine, my uncle wanted to talk to Sunita, and again, he couldn't think of anything to say. As soon as he was within earshot, he questioned her, "Why your parents don't buy *Graphic*? It more soft than *Chronicle*."

Once again, he was impressed by Sunita's wit as she quipped, "I gon give you sand-paper next time."

This process continued for a few weeks until Ramlall rode under the house one day to find Sunita's father, Mangal, lying in the hammock under the house. Mangal had gotten wind of the situation, and decided to come home early from his farm, to protect his daughter's reputation. A thin, wiry man, with a large moustache, Mangal did not change from his work-clothes, covered with dust and sweat. He had not shaved for a week, and as he rose from his hammock, and wiped the sweat off his face, Ramlall was intimidated, even though he was younger and stronger.

Mangal faced Ramlall, whose urge to go to the latrine somehow seemed less urgent. He did not waste any words as he looked Ramlall directly in the eyes. "You only want to go to the latrine when you reach the house Sunita live in. You gon marry her, or you gon shit somewhere else?"

Quite suddenly, Ramlall's bowels seemed at the point of releasing, and the only reply he could think of was, "I really got to go to the latrine," as he grabbed a sheet of *The Chronicle* lying on a chair, and escaped along the dirt path.

As he squatted in the latrine, Ramlall had time to think about the situation. If the truth be told, he was glad that things were being brought to this point. He was completely captivated by Sunita, and wanted to marry her, but was unsure how to proceed. *Ah gon tell him to speak to my big brother about it*, he thought. *Since our father died, he act as father to all of us.*

When Ramlall approached the bottom house, Mangal was still standing, leaning against a house post, a Bristol cigarette hanging from his lips. Ramlall did not even look in his direction, but went directly to the standpipe, and took his time to wash his hands. Then he glanced at the kitchen attached to the house, and saw Sunita smiling seductively at him. This gave him some courage, and he walked quickly to Mangal.

"You got to talk to my brother, Babu, and *ask for me.*[39]"

Mangal took this as a sign of consent, and told Ramlall, "All right! Tell Babu that I gon come on Saturday night and ask home for you. Sunita is a good girl. She can cook, and she learn sewing. She doesn't walk brazen like some a dem girl who don't have no shame. She down she head when she walk."

And she got nice breasts too, Ramlall thought.

Mangal was true to his word, and went to my father the following Saturday to propose that Ramlall marry Sunita. My father and Ramlall agreed, and the date for the wedding was set. Leaves of water lilies were cut to serve as plates, rice was boiled, and the many helpers cooked dhal and curried potatoes, among other dishes. The *bariat*[40] set out to Sunita's house, and the pundit performed the Hindu ceremony.

Then the pundit handed Ramlall the legal marriage papers. "You and Sunita only got to sign this, and we finished."

---

[39] Propose marriage.
40 People accompanying the bridegroom to the wedding, usually held at the bride's residence.

Mangal was astonished when Ramlall told the pundit, "You married us already. We gon sign the papers later."

"The gal ain't leaving this house if you don't sign the papers," Mangal threatened.

"But the pundit married us already," Ramlall countered.

"Sign the papers, or else the gal staying just heah," Mangal emphasized, as he extended his index finger and made a jabbing motion to the ground.

Ramlall thought of the disappointment faced by his relatives and friends if he returned home without a bride to show for all their efforts in arranging his wedding. He realized he was outmaneuvered, and reluctantly took the pen from the pundit and signed the marriage papers. The pundit then handed the papers to Sunita, who signed them with a flourish. They would later be submitted to the Office of the Registrar General, in Georgetown, to legalize the marriage.

When the wedding party returned to our home, the bride was accompanied by two *Luknis*[41]. In the Hindu tradition, a marriage is not consummated until the second Sunday, and a Lukni is sent with the bride. The bride would return to her parents' home the following day, and the groom would bring his bride home the next Sunday—referred to as *Second Sunday*. The marriage would then be consummated. Usually, only one *Lukni* was required, but for one reason or another, Sunita's mother felt that her daughter needed extra protection.

When Ramlall returned to our home with his bride, the usual ceremonies were performed, with my mother welcoming Sunita to our home. Then the Luknis and Sunita retired to a bedroom, which was prepared by my mother and my sisters, and guests lined up to present money to the bride in order to *see*[42] her.

Ramlall, still peeved that he had lost the fight about signing the legal papers, went downstairs and had quite a few drinks with his

---

[41] Custodians who ensured the bride remained virtuous until she was officially brought to the groom's house on the Second Sunday.

[42] It was customary for invitees to present money to the bride in order to meet her.

friends and relatives. The alcohol fueled his desire for Sunita, and determined to assert himself, he headed straight to the room where Sunita and the two Luknis were seated on the bed. Everybody had already met the bride so, the room was empty, except for Sunita and the Luknis. Sunita looked even more beautiful and desirable in her wedding dress.

Ramlall's desire became more intense, and he turned to one Lukni. "You signed for the girl?"

The Lukni, unaware of where the conversation was going, retorted, "I didn't marry none girl. Why I gon sign for the girl?"

Ramlall turned to the other Lukni and repeated the question.

The Lukni was indignant. "How I gon sign? I can't read or write. My mother and father never send me to school, or else who gon do the housework?"

Ramlall was tired of all the verbiage. "You sign for the girl, Yes or No?"

"I can't write English, how I gon sign?" Then seeing that Ramlall was getting extremely red in the face, she simply said, "No!"

Ramlall, speaking louder this time, told both Luknis, "If none of you sign fuh the girl, then get out. I sign fuh the girl." He practically pushed the Luknis out of the room and bolted the door.

The conversation was heard by most of the people in the hall, in spite of the rather loud music. The men and some of the younger women were bemused, while some of the older women made tutting sounds.

One old woman muttered loudly enough so that those near her could hear, "He don't have no shame."

When the creaking of the bed was heard even above the loud music, my father tactfully went to the juke box, and turned up the volume to the highest.

24 STORMING THE GAME by Ram Jagessar

Iwitnessed a historic storming one day in the sixties when Naparima College played the annual grudge match against Presentation College in Skinner Park. It was south intercollegiate with a vengeance and interest and rivalry were intense. I kid you not.

We, the Naparima boys, were packed into one of the stands reserved for us, screaming insults at the Presentation boys crammed in the other stand. A huge standing-room crowd filled the grounds area after paying an entry fee—Intercol was not free, you know!

At the wire fence, seven or eight feet high, another crowd of young men who had no money to buy entry into the park, were determined to storm the Intercol event by climbing the fence and joining the standing room crowd in the grounds area. Keeping the stormers at bay, several policemen were positioned just inside the fence. Their leader, a police inspector in khaki, stood close to the Naparima College stand.

As we waited for the match to start, we had nothing to do but watch the drama unfold, as stormers climbed the fence in the gap between the policemen, jumped down and dashed into the grounds, evading the cops to great applause and laughter from us, and eventually melting into the crowd for safety in numbers.

Police, unable to get them once they were blended in the crowd, tried to nab them as they ran the gauntlet from the fence. It was highly entertaining, and as you can imagine, the Naparima stand was all in sympathy with the stormers, and against the police.

One or two brave stormers took their chances, climbed the fence like circus monkeys, jumped down the other side and raced into the grounds, evading the frustrated cops who were clearly not enjoying their failures.

Then, one young fellow took his chance in the gap between the inspector and a constable, and ran up the fence, intending to flip over the top, drop on the ground, sprint into the crowd away from the advancing inspector. But alas, the mount was good, the descent not so good. The fold in his right leg jeans caught in the wire at the top of the fence and instead of dropping on his feet he flopped head down, feet up, hanging helplessly upside down on the wire fence.

A gale of laughter swept the Naparima stand, and yes, the waiting stormers on the other side of the fence and even the grounds crowd who turned to watch the spectacle. The failed stormer tried frantically to push himself up and release his jeans from the wire, which only increased the laughter. He couldn't do it; his full weight on the wire was too much to counter his upside-down position.

The inspector stood his position, hands on hips, wryly shaking his head. He wasn't laughing. Finally, he walked up to the trapped stormer, now hanging frozen, as he knew he couldn't escape by himself. Inspector went up to him, held him by the waist, lifted him up so his jeans were freed from the wire, flipped him over and gently placed him feet first on the ground.

A gust of appreciative applause went through Skinner Park by all who witnessed this act of kindness. Then, the inspector pointed his finger at the fence and told the stormer in sign language to climb back over. And the interloper did so, slowly, to more ripples of laughter as he dropped down on the ground and melted away, his storming day ending in humiliation.

After that the Intercol game was an anti-climax, and yes, Naparima lost again, but we went back to Paradise Hill chanting, "We go win next year."

25 HOW I TRAUMATIZED MY COUSIN by Kennard Ramphal

I was four years older than my cousin, Ram, who was, and still is one of my favorite cousins. He was the son of *Coot Mamoo*, my mother's brother, and they lived in the rice farming village of Windsor Forest, on the west coast of Demerara.

International travel was unknown to us, and for our holiday treats, we visited Windsor Forest, to spend time with our cousins. Likewise, they visited us in Canal Number 2, the farming village in which we lived, as part of their holidays. The close relationship between us and our cousins was as intimate as the one we had with our siblings, and the times we spent together were golden moments of pleasure.

In the summer of my sixteenth year, everybody was overjoyed when we saw Ram, suitcase in hand, walking across the bridge spanning the canal to our home. The single road in our village was on the north side of the drainage canal, and a number of bridges provided access to the houses on the south side.

Ram was tall for his age, almost as tall as I was, and sported a perpetual smile on his face. I really liked and admired him, and endeavored to earn his complete trust, because he demonstrated a deep regard for the well-being of others that was far advanced for his age. During his visits to Canal, I endeavored to make his stay as enjoyable as possible, and we picked whatever fruits were in season, either from our farm, or our neighbors' farms. Most afternoons were spent swimming in the black, sweet water of the conservancy canal, about a mile from our village.

My father had one of the few shotguns in our village, and the meat he provided by hunting acouris,[43] ducks, and anakwahs[44] was a welcome addition to our diet of mostly rice or roti, and some sort of curried vegetables. When I turned fifteen, my father had trusted me enough to allow me to hunt with our shotgun, and I endeavored to earn his trust by contributing a few acouris and anakwahs to the family diet.

One afternoon, Dhanraj, a friend of about my age, and who enjoyed telling jokes and playing pranks, visited me, and we decided to take Ram hunting in the forest south of our home. Ram was very excited to go with us, and told his aunt, my mother, "We gon bring home an accouri, or a duck Aunty."

With high hopes, we set out on the path between the coffee trees, keeping our eyes peeled for anakwahs nesting among the thick branches of the trees. We saw none of the birds and emerged from our coffee farm to enter the jungle at the back of the farm, named *Hampa Bush* by the villagers. However, it was not our day to shoot any game, and after about an hour's hike, we were still in the forest, walking softly along the path, looking for an accouri or any edible bird. I badly wanted to show my cousin how good a shot I was, and became frustrated and disappointed when it began to get dark, and we hadn't succeeded.

Up to this day, I cannot explain why I decided to play a trick on my beloved cousin, who had absolute trust in me and whose company I always thoroughly enjoyed. In retrospect, I think that I had attempted to compensate for my lack of success in finding some sort of game, and my failure to understand the long-term consequences of my actions.

"I think that we're lost," I said.

Dhanraj caught on immediately. "We have to sleep in the bush," he said, looking at Ram, who remained stoically quiet, and was probably confident that his cousin would protect him.

When I saw that our ploy was thus far effective, I decided to increase the dose. "We have to sleep in the trees," I added. "But we have to sleep in different trees, so that if a tiger should come, it will

---

43 A type of rabbit
44 A tasty bird, somewhat like the partridge

eat only one of us. It will probably choose the smallest one."

When my cousin started crying, I immediately relented and tried to reassure him. "Don't worry, Ram. We were just joking."

However, he kept on crying intermittently, and was still sobbing when we reached home. My mother must have wondered why he ate so little at dinner that night. The following morning, everything appeared to be normal. Ram spent a few more days before returning to Windsor Forest, and I forgot all about the incident.

In adult life, Ram joined the police force, and I enlisted in the army where we both had successful careers. Years later, the politics of Guyana encouraged both of us to leave the country, Ram to the United States, and I to Toronto. After a few years of struggle, we were relatively successful in our adopted countries.

One Christmas, more than fifty years after the incident described above, there was a reunion of myself, my brother, Dwarka, and his wife, Rita, in Ram's house in Miami, Florida. Dwarka and Rita had travelled from North Carolina to be with us. Apart from the pleasure of meeting my brother, his wife, and my cousin, it was very refreshing for me to escape from a minus twelve-degree weather in Toronto to a plus twenty-two-degree climate. We were relaxing on the very comfortable porch at the back of Ram's house enjoying the third drink of El Dorado fifteen-year-old, and smoking Cohiba cigars.

Ram turned to me and said, earnestly, "Bud, you were my best cousin, but I still remember how you traumatized me."

"What do you mean, Ram? I always looked out for you."

"Remember when you and Dhanraj took me hunting? And you told me that we were lost, and that we would have to sleep in trees? And you emphasized that we would have to sleep in different trees, so that if a tiger comes, it would eat only one of us? That thing is still traumatizing me."

I recalled the incident, which was meant as a harmless prank, and it never occurred to me that it would have caused such long-lasting trauma. I apologized profusely to my dear cousin, knowing that no apology could erase the pain that I inflicted on him.

That conversation with Ram reinforced the fact that actions and words have lasting consequences. Activists warn people that, when you say or do something, "It's not the intent that matters. It's the impact that the words and actions have on others."

My cousin revealed to me the harmful and long-term effects of my foolish actions in my salad days, and I have learnt a valuable lesson.

26 GOOM GOOM'S MARRIAGE by Ram Jagessar

My father's drinking buddy, Goom Goom, was serious about two things in life—drinking my daddy's rum, and his marriage. He is dead now—Goom Goom I mean—and I can tell the seriously sad story about how his two loves got him into trouble.

Every morning my father, a serious alcoholic in his forties, would call on Goom Goom to share a bottle or two at Lovey Rum Shop, and his faithful servant would dutifully answer the command.

By noon, Daddy would be soused to the gills, and Goom Goom would take him home, carry him upstairs and put him in the bed to sleep it off. He would repeat the joyful task later if my father was up to a second round.

This meant, of course, that Goom wasn't earning any money to keep up his household, and was seriously neglecting his wife, Meena. Now Meena was a tall, attractive, very shapely, very fair woman, almost like them Bollywood film stars, and she didn't have to put up with her husband's lack of attention. Finally, she got fed up, and moved out to shack up with another feller.

Big problem!

The new feller was a creole, or *Kilwal*, as the common expression was. I doubt any of us knew what the word meant back then. Today, they would say a Black man.

Goom knew that the new feller was treating Meena bad, and he could take a little horn, but not if the man was a creole. No shame was worse than that.

He started drinking even more of my father rum and crying in the shot glass that the wife bring him shame and disgrace. He told me he couldn't take it no more but he didn't know what to do.

Couldn't go and beg Meena to come back because he didn't have money to give the woman. Besides, she was already spoiled by going with the Kilwal.

One day, he tell me he decide to kill heself to end his shame, hang himself from one of my father cocoa tree. He looked around for a good strong rope to make the hangman knot, but no rope was to be found. No goat rope, no cow rope to be found. All he could find was some bag twine they used to tie the cocoa bag when my father was selling dry cocoa by the Chinese man shop.

That would have to do. He doubled up the bag twine about six times, finish off the whole roll, and end up with a kind of thin rope. That should do the job.

Goom went in Daddy's cocoa estate and climb up one of them big, tall cocoa tree, the kind that will reach 30 feet or more. He step out on one of them thick branch, put the hangman knot around he neck, and tie the other end around the branch and jump off.

Badap! The rope twine snap like a rotten branch and Goom drop hard on his bottom bone on a cocoa root sticking out of the ground and a terrible pain run through him like a 400-volt electric shock.

"Oh God O! She could take ten creole man now!" he groaned.

Maybe she did. But Goom was a changed man. I don't know how he did it, but he got Meena to come back, and after my father died from drinking too much rum, the two moved to my uncle Hanuman's house after he, too, died of drinking too much rum.

Uncle Sook, alias Cap, was taking care of the house and estate, and Cap needed a main drinking buddy. Goom was well qualified to handle that job.

Turned out, Meena liked to take a nip or two of rum with Goom and Cap, and a good time was had by all for a while though Goom was not totally happy with his excessive drinking. He went to see the pundit.

Pundit tell him, "If you have to drink, drink in murderation,[45]

---

[45] He meant in moderation.

beta."

Pundits in those days didn't have much English education so you have to forgive they mistake.

One evening Goom beat Meena to death with a scrubbing board when he was so drunk, he didn't know what he was doing. He got serious jail time for manslaughter, and on his return went back to hanging out with Uncle Cap, who was carrying on the family tradition of drinking too much rum.

Goom would take a lil nip or two, but he never went back to crazy man drinking of the scrubbing board style.

27 FORGETFUL ABEL by Kennard Ramphal

Our entire household was overjoyed when my brother, Jai, who was eighteen months older than I was, was hired as a pupil teacher in Affiance Methodist School after being baptized by the Methodist minister. The Christian name he had chosen was Abel. Before his baptism, we had all called him Jai, an abbreviation of his Hindu name, Jewarhirlall, and we had to get accustomed to his Christian name. Through an inexplicable process, over time, we addressed him by only by his Christian name. The notable exceptions were Ma and Daddy, who continued to call him, Jai.

Affiance was a small village on the Essequibo coast, and because we lived in the rural village of Canal No. 2 Polder, on the west bank of the Demerara River, Abel had to ride his bicycle to Vreed-en-hoop, after asking one of the friendly hire-car drivers to take his heavy suitcase and leave it at Choo's Cake Shop, located near the train and ferry station. After collecting his suitcase, Abel had to take the train to Parika, then board the ferry across the Essequibo River to Suddie, and finally cycle for five miles to Affiance. It required a full day of travel, and therefore the only times that Abel was able to visit home was during the Christmas, Easter, and of course the summer holidays. Daddy had arranged for Abel to board and lodge with one of his friends, Ramroop, for a modest amount of money. Ramroop, who owned a cake shop, lived in a convenient location, about a twenty-minute ride from Affiance Methodist School.

This meant that Abel had to pack all his books and every-day stuff needed for about three months. This posed a constant challenge because Abel's head was always in the clouds. This is a kind way of saying that he was very forgetful.

In September 1957 Abel, a pampered fifteen-year-old, who had never been away from home for any significant length of time, packed his suitcase, and asked Ma's first cousin, Budya, a hire car driver, to drop his suitcase to Choo's. Abel jumped on his bicycle and began his journey to his first teaching stint.

Three days after Abel left, a postman arrived at our home, leaned his bicycle against the coconut tree in front of our home, and handed Ma a telegram. Ma could read and write Hindi fluently, but not English, so she passed the telegram to Daddy, who signed for it. Before reading the telegram, he opened the kerosene fridge we kept in our grocery store and took out a cold bottle of Pepsi, which he handed to the sweating postman, who accepted it gratefully. As the postman was drinking the Pepsi, Daddy looked the telegram.

Ma anxiously said, "What the telegram say?"

Daddy glanced at the telegram and then looked at Ma. "It is from Jai. The telegram say, PLEASE POST RAINCOAT." Daddy's face reflected both frustration and amusement. He was frustrated because he knew that he would have to be the one to go to Wales Post Office and post the raincoat, and he was amused because he and Ma were always joking about how forgetful Abel was. "Jai always forgetting something. Now he forget his raincoat, and he asking us to post it," he elaborated.

Ma was surprised that Daddy, who always stuttered when he was upset or excited, did not stutter on this occasion. "I sorry that he get a teaching job so far. I don't want rain to wet him and make him catch cold. I gon put the raincoat in a box, and you take it to the post office tomorrow. I gon work with the laborers in the farm."

"I got to waste a whole day to post the raincoat for him."

"They don't have any store in Affiance he can buy a raincoat from," Ma replied soothingly. "You go and post the raincoat. Don't worry about the laborers. I gon work with them."

In order to discourage Daddy from complaining further, she immediately left, took a box from our grocery store, and folded Abel's mackintosh raincoat so that it could fit in the box. She put the raincoat in the box, sealed it securely with masking tape, and wrapped some strong twine around it. She tied the string securely, and turned to Daddy. "You got Ramroop's address? You got to write the address on the box."

Daddy went upstairs to the table we used for reading and

writing, selected a pen, and came down to write Abel's name and Ramroop's address on the brown box. The following morning, Ma went with the laborers to weed the coffee farm, while Daddy jumped on his Humber bicycle and rode the nine miles to Wales Post Office, where he posted the box. I wish Jai make sure that he pack everything before he leave. Look how much trouble he give me, he thought as he cycled back home.

As he approached Inderdai's rum shop, Daddy thought, The day spoil already. Lemme make a bad job of it, and he steered his bicycle into the path leading to her shop. Inderdai was his sister, so he spent some time catching up on family matters before he ordered a quarter bottle of El Dorado rum.

The reader who is familiar with rum shop etiquette will not need any explanation why Daddy invited Bhai Bhai, a close friend of his, to have a drink with him as soon as he entered the rum shop. He will also understand why other friends who walked into the rum shop would have invited Daddy and Bhai Bhai to have a drink with them. When the bottle they were drinking from was finished, the reader will understand why Bhai Bhai felt that it was his turn to buy a bottle. Rum shop etiquette would dictate that he buy a large bottle when there were five people at the table. The result was that Daddy, totally inebriated, went home at about one in the morning.

Ma understood that he was frustrated at losing a whole day's work at the farm, and didn't say anything when he came home wasted, although she knew that he would miss work next day also.

As he slid into bed, she said, "You post the raincoat fuh Jai?"

"Yes. Then I drop in at Inderdai for a quick quarter. Bhai Bhai drop in, and I say it gon look bad not to invite him for a drink, so I tell him to come and tek a drink with me. Then Baba and Googol and Sunil come in."

Daddy would have given a detailed account of the night's proceedings, but even in his intoxicated state, he noticed that Ma was already snoring. Feeling deprived that he did not get an opportunity to tell the entire story, he had no option but to snuggle up to his wife, before falling asleep.

Abel wrote intermittent letters telling us how he was getting on in school, and although we missed him, everybody was happy that he got a teaching job, and was doing well. Before we knew it, Christmas holidays loomed, and everybody was overjoyed when Abel came home. The trouble Daddy took to post the raincoat was forgotten amid the celebrations and gift giving, until it was time for Abel to return to Affiance. Abel asked Polo, who drove a blue Vauxhall hire car, to take his suitcase to Vreed-en-hoop, and Ma cried as he jumped on his bicycle to start his day-long journey.

On the second day after he left, it was raining, and Ma and Daddy were surprised to see a figure approaching our house in a raincoat—people would not venture out in the rain unless it was very important. As the person approached, Daddy's face mirrored all kinds of emotions as he recognized the postman who had delivered the earlier telegram. Wordlessly, the postman, who was understandably upset at having to come out in that weather, pulled out a waterproof bag from under his coat, extracted a telegram and a receipt, which he handed to Daddy, and pointed to the place where Daddy had to sign. Daddy signed the receipt, and handed it back to the postman, who looked at him expectantly, anticipating the offer of another Pepsi. But Daddy was experiencing too many emotions to think about mundane things like Pepsi, so the disappointed postman left. Daddy held the telegram in his hand for a long time, and Ma anxiously waited for him to read the contents.

"You gon open it, or what?" she said.

Daddy opened the telegram. "PLEASE POST LONG BOOTS," he read to her. Both looked at each other wordlessly for quite a few minutes.

Ma, surprised that Daddy did not stutter, broke the silence. "I really sorry for Jai." She placed her hand on Daddy's arm to placate him. "Munny and Dhanraj get teaching jobs close to home. Dhanraj can come home every day, and Munny can come home every Friday. But Jai teaching so far away." She looked at Daddy with tears in her eyes as he remained wordless, before she continued, "I gon go and put the long boots in a box so you can post it tomorrow." She then went in our grocery store to select a suitable box, leaving Daddy in a dazed state.

Daddy went to the post office the following day and posted the long boots, and Abel continued to write letters informing us of his progress, and his intention to stay in Affiance for the Easter holidays, to study for the Pupil Teachers' First Year Examination in June.

In June, when Abel was about to leave Affiance to write the exams, his headmaster, a kind sixty-year-old man who was near retirement, told him that he did not need to return to school after the exams to teach just a few days before the school closed for the summer break. He indicated that he would give Abel a few days leave so that he could start enjoying the summer holidays early.

We had foreknowledge of Abel's arrival in June when Polo dropped his suitcase off at our home, but there was no time for celebrations when he arrived, sweating on his bicycle, because our exams were on the following day. Both Abel and I went to write our teachers' exam, and when the results were published in the local newspapers in mid-July, we were happy to learn that we both passed.

The summer holidays just flew by, and soon it was time for Abel to start packing. "All of you say that I always forget something," he repeatedly told us as he packed to leave for over three months once again. "This time, I will not forget anything," he emphasized as he folded his raincoat, and put it in his suitcase.

Then he put his long boots in a large paper bag which Daddy had brought from Bookers Stores. He checked and double checked that his ties, belts, shirts and trousers were packed. Sunday arrived too soon, and Abel joined Budya's hire-car to begin his journey.

Two days after Abel left, Ma and Daddy saw the familiar sight of a postman on the way to our house. "What he forget this time?" Daddy said as the postman came to the door. The postman handed over the telegram and the receipt. Daddy accepted them wordlessly.

Ma meanwhile was thinking, I help him pack his raincoat, his long boots, all his shirts and ties, his handkerchiefs, everything. What he forget now?

As Daddy opened the telegram, Ma was anxiously leaning forward. Then Daddy started stuttering as he read, *P-PLEASE P-POST B-BICYCLE.*

28 A CORTINA WINDSHIELD AND BAD DREAMS by Ram Jagessar

My cousin, Betty, tell me years ago that his father Cortina car windshield get hit with a stone and a hole appear, so they knew new windshield was necessary. Father was working, so he couldn't go to get it fix. He mention it to Betty, who say he will look into it.

Same day, Betty talk to he pardner, Gulgul, about where to buy a windshield and pardner say, "Doh buy it, I will get one for you free! I will come tonight with the windshield."

Betty like the sound of free!

Ten o'clock in the night, the pardner Gulgul come with another pardner and say, "Leh we go for the windshield."

"You ain't bring it?" Betty axe him.

Pardner say," We have to pick it up! Jump in."

So off they go.

Driving in a residential area with cars parked up on the road, pardner asking Betty, "Is your Cortina like that one?"

Betty say, "Nah, earlier model," and they drive on.

Finally, Betty see a Cortina like he father model and say "Is one like that!"

Creeks! Car pull up next to the good windshield Cortina. The pardner and he pardner jump out and open up the trunk, pull out two tools, each one looking like a toilet plunger tie up on a stick.

Betty say to heself, "They going to clear up toilet ten o'clock in the night?"

The two pardners go to both sides of the Cortina windshield, slam down the plunger tools on the glass and they stick: *Blap*!

Chief pardner, Gulgul, say "One, two, three, pull!" and the two of them pull and the whole windshield come out, *Floops*! in their hand, and they run and drop it in the trunk, jump in the car and say, "Come leh we go Sookie. Come leh we go!"

Betty sit down in the car, he eyes bug out, gasping like he just get baptize three times under water in the Caroni River.

"Why you looking at me funny so?" axe Gulgul.

"I didn't know you was going to thief the windshield," he stammer.

"How the fork you will get windshield for free if you doh thief it?" pardner explain.

Betty say no more. Now he understand whey they call the pardner Gulgul.

They went home by he and put on the windshield same speed as when they thief it.

Next morning Betty father pleased as bald head Gokool when he get a bottle of Rogaine. Betty father ask him, "How you get a windshield so quick?"

"I got some good pardner," say Betty, and nothing more.

That night, and every night, Betty father getting bad dream about the car. "I dreaming about the Cortina, and that somebody thief something from the car," the daddy saying.

Betty ain't say nothing. What you doh know cyah hurt you.

29 DRINKING CERVEZAS AT THE PEGASUS by Kennard Ramphal

"How about some beers at the Pegasus?" Roy, scion of a wealthy window manufacturer, told me and my brothers, Abel, and Balram, as he patted his well-padded wallet with his right hand.

A six-footer, who exuded confidence with his booming voice, and long beard, Roy was drinking rum and coke with us at my newly built home in Meadowbrook Gardens. We jumped at the offer. Pegasus was the newest, most upscale hotel and restaurant in Georgetown, and indeed in Guyana. I might add that it was also the most expensive one.

Roy scowled when Abel and Balram refused his offer to ride in his brand-new blue Ford pick-up truck, and instead elected to join me in my old Mini-Cooper, thus denying him the pleasure of showing off his vehicle. We lost sight of the Ford as Roy weaved through traffic, and even drove through a red light, the powerful engine of the Ford allowing him to leave us comfortably behind, as my Mini-Cooper sputtered along, and strained to gain momentum after we stopped at traffic lights.

When we pulled into the parking lot of the tall and majestic Pegasus overlooking the Atlantic Ocean, we spotted Roy by the entrance of the hotel, his right hand in his pocket, apparently holding his wallet, and we felt grateful that he invited us for beers at a very prestigious hotel.

As we started to walk towards the hotel, I thought that it was an excellent opportunity to practice Spanish with Balram, who had graduated from the University of Guyana a few years earlier. I had recently enrolled at that university, and constantly questioned why students were required to take either Spanish or French as a required course. Having had no exposure to Spanish before enrolment, I was having problems learning this language, and I felt that I was not ready for the exam to be held in a month.

I greeted Roy with, "Hola amigo," but after he gave me a puzzled look, I turned to Balram, my younger brother a fair, handsome guy of about twenty-three, who was clean-shaven, with his long, black hair neatly combed, and his shoes always polished with a shine. It was a puzzle to all his friends how he managed to keep his shoes so clean, even when the roads were muddy. If the truth be told, he was once told by a girl with whom he was deeply infatuated, that she could always tell the quality of a guy by looking at his hair and his shoes. From that day on, Balram ensured that he had an adequate supply of Brillantine hair gel, and polished his shoes every day. He even kept a cloth in his back pocket to wipe them ever so often.

"Como estas?" I said to Balram, as we made our way to the lounge.

Balram looked at his shoes before replying, "Muy bien, gracias."

When the waiter arrived, I was so anxious to practice my Spanish, that I forgot that it was Roy who had invited us, and therefore it was his right to order.

"Cuatro cervezas por favor," I ordered, in what I hoped was good Spanish.

The waiter apparently knew, or at least, understood Spanish, and left immediately to fetch us the beers, as Balram and I continued conversing in that language. When Roy, feeling totally sidelined, abruptly left without saying a word to anyone, Balram and I continued our Spanish dialogue, unperturbed.

Abel, tall and lean, and older than I by eighteen months, sat at the table looking intensely at me and Balram. It was the first time he had been at the Pegasus, and was understandably frustrated and upset that his brothers insisted in speaking a language he did not understand. When the waiter eventually arrived and put four beers on the table, he reached for a beer and started sipping it without saying a word.

"Muy bien cerveza," I observed to Balram as I sipped the cold beer.

"Si," Balram responded. "Mas major que el ron," indicating that the beer was better than rum.

Abel was silent as he looked sullenly around the lounge, where several seemingly well-to-do people were enjoying their drinks. Balram and I were busy practicing our Spanish but I still noticed Abel's hand shaking slightly as he raised his beer to his mouth.

We finished our beers, and were in the process of sharing the fourth beer intended for Roy, when the waiter approached and asked me—I was the person who ordered the first round, "Would you like another round, sir?"

I would have liked another beer, but remembered that I had no money, and the person whose pockets were always bulging was no longer with us.

"Nada," I told the waiter.

"That will be fifteen dollars," the waiter said.

"Quince dollars" I told Balram. "Tiene usted dinero?"

"No tengo dinero," Balram replied, and we both looked at Abel, earnestly hoping that he had at least fifteen dollars.

After an uncomfortable silence, Abel looked at me squarely with his intense eyes and replied, "You ordered them in Spanish. Pay for them in English," as he leaned back in his chair.

I immediately forgot to speak in Spanish. "I don't have any money," I told him.

"You ordered them in Spanish. Pay for them in English," Abel repeated, with what appeared to be a smirk.

The waiter immediately sensed that there was going to be a problem. He went behind the counter, picked up a phone, dialed a number, and then hung up. In a few minutes, a burly guy with long hair and a beard appeared and initiated a conversation with the waiter.

"That's security," I told Balram and Abel, as I reached into my pocket, pulled out my cheque book, and motioned to the waiter. "I just remembered that I have my cheque book. I can write you a cheque." After the waiter hesitated, I emphasized, "In English," as I flashed my cheque book.

"You should have told us that before you ordered. We can do nothing when you walk out of here, and your cheque bounces." The waiter raised his voice and looked at security as he spoke. By then, the other patrons in the lounge were staring at us.

Abel observed everything with a smile, and obviously enjoyed seeing me sweat. At that time, there were no visa cards, and no ATM machines, so it appeared as we were doomed to be embarrassed.

"Well, I have only my cheque book and no money, so what do you want me to do?" I said to the waiter.

By this time, the security guard had approached our table, and addressed me directly. "We're going to call the police," he said. "It is fraud if you order drinks, knowing that you have no money to pay for them."

He started to walk towards the phone when Abel interrupted. "How much did you say the bill was?"

"Fifteen dollars," the waiter said, as the security guy hesitated.

I breathed a loud sigh of relief as Abel pulled out a roll of bills, counted fifteen dollars, and handed the cash to the waiter, who accepted it with a scowl and returned to his place behind the bar.

You had the money all this time, and you made us sweat, I thought, as I looked at Abel with a mixture of gratitude and frustration. We avoided looking at the other customers, and quickly left the hotel and hastened towards my Mini-Cooper in order to distance ourselves from the source of our discomfort.

As I turned the key in the ignition and the engine sputtered, Abel turned to me smugly and asked, "Are we going back to your place to drink some rum, or do you have any dinero to buy more cervezas?"

30 GIVING UP MY FIRST PAY by Ram Jagessar

I distinctly remember my shock when my mother suggested I give my first paycheque to my father. I had gotten my first job teaching at ASJA Boys' College in San Fernando at the age of 19 and was proud as any fowl cock at earning my own money.

And here was Ma saying give the whole thing to Daddy! Ridiculous. I would be penniless. But she was insistent.

Most reluctantly, I came up to Daddy and offered him the cheque just like Whoopi Goldberg in the movie, *Ghost*, offering the $4 million cheque to the Catholic nun.

He took it, looked at it for a long moment, swallowed hard and tears came to his eyes.

Then he hugged me and gave back the cheque without a word.

I didn't understand, but my mother did.

It was one of those perfect moments in time that I will never forget.

31 ABEL AND WHAT MAKES IT TICK by Kennard Ramphal

During the summer holidays, my elder brother, Abel, and I learned that we had passed the Pupil Teachers' Second Year Examination and we were on Cloud Nine.

Abel was five feet, ten inches tall, thin as a broomstick, and tired of people teasing him about his leanness. Consequently, in preparation for the summer holidays, he had ordered a Charles Atlas course by mail. BUILD YOUR BODY IN JUST TEN MINUTES A DAY, the advertisement had proclaimed. The blurb explained how Charles Atlas was a ninety-seven-pound weakling, and when some hoodlums kicked sand in his face and in the face of his girlfriend, poor Charles could not stand up to them. He was so traumatized by the incident that he developed a number of body building exercises. When the exercises resulted in Charles Atlas being named THE WORLD'S MOST PERFECTLY DEVELOPED MAN, he decided to share his secrets with the world for a modest fee.

Abel and I attempted to follow the instructions mailed to us, and our exercises included push-ups, using two chairs, and pull-ups on one of the low branches of the orange trees surrounding our house. After two weeks, the only difference we saw, or rather felt, was consistent and nagging pain in our pectoral and arm muscles, and other muscles that we didn't even know that we had.

At the same time that we decided to abandon the Charles Atlas course, our parents were involved in picking coffee berries from our farm, and they had hired some young women from our village to help. Abel and I decided to help our parents pick coffee, and managed to convince ourselves that the beautiful, full breasted girls our parents hired did not at all influence our decision.

"We gon come and help you and Daddy pick coffee tomorrow,"

Abel told Ma, as we sat down to a dinner of curried boulangers and potatoes and roti.

"Good," Ma told him. "The coffee so ripe that it falling, and we have to pick them up from the ground. But the coffee farm got so much bush that we can't get all the coffee from the ground. You got to wake up early if you gon come and help."

"All right Ma! Wake me and Dhanraj up early."

"Okay! I gon wake you up. You gon help us until we finish picking all the coffee? I notice that you start so many things, but you don't finish them."

"We gon help you pick coffee until you finish picking all the coffee, Ma. We on holidays."

"So, you say," Ma replied skeptically.

Although she loved her second son dearly, Ma also knew that Abel abandoned many projects as soon as he became interested in others. She and Daddy also recognized that Abel had an inquisitive mind, and was interested in what made things tick. He would often take things apart, and then discover that he couldn't reassemble them.

The following morning, Ma woke us up early, and after breakfast, we set off with her, Daddy and the three girls she had hired. Ma and Daddy had picked coffee from the trees nearest our house earlier and decided to start the day at the perimeter of our coffee farm. When we reached the end of our farm, Ma gave Abel and me a thick cloth. We knew the drill, and tied one end of the cloth around our waists, then tucked the loose ends in the one around our waist to create a small bag to put the coffee berries. There were baskets, placed along the path to empty our bags when they were full.

Between the end of our farm and the end of our property, there was a large patch of land which was half-swamp. The land in Canal No. 2 was *pegasse*, consisting mostly of decaying leaves and plants. This made it very fertile, but it also made it burn easily. An earlier fire had burnt this patch of land transforming it into a swamp, making it unsuitable for coffee cultivation. Abel climbed a tree and picked the ripe coffee berries from a branch. Then he looked at the burnt piece of land and started to contemplate.

"All that land is going to waste," he said. "We can plant rice on that land. But if nobody else plants rice, birds will eat all of our paddy. We have to encourage all the neighbors to also plant rice, so birds will eat a little from each farm, and we will still get enough to make a profit."

He then planned how to encourage the neighbors, how to prepare the land, and how to irrigate it. In fact, he explored all the aspects of rice cultivation and marketing.

We were quite a few rows ahead when Abel emptied his pouch containing about fifty berries in a basket. "I am going home," he announced.

Because he was a volunteer and not a laborer, Ma and Daddy couldn't object, but as soon as Abel was out of earshot, Daddy made a prediction—loud enough for everyone to hear, "Either the clock or the radio gone."

Daddy was referring to the large wall clock, which my eldest brother, John, had bought when he had passed his Third-Class Teachers' examination. Clocks and watches were not very prevalent in Canal in those days, and we were so proud of it that we kept our windows open, even when it was raining, so that people walking on the road could see what time it was. Another of our prized possessions was our radio, also uncommon in Canal at that time. We accommodated requests by neighbors to turn the volume up during the time when Radio Demerara played Indian songs, and death announcements.

At the end of the workday, we loaded the wicker baskets full of coffee berries into the *corial*,[46] and pulled the boat in the four-foot drain which led straight to our home. Once we were home, we unloaded the berries from the corial, and placed them in a heap. Later, we would pass the berries through a grinder to split the pulp, so that they could dry more easily. Daddy would then take the dried coffee berries to *Coffee Baba*, Ma's cousin, who owned one of the two

---

46 Long, narrow boat

factories in our village, to separate the beans from the pulp.

After we finished unloading the *corial*, Daddy washed his hands and feet, went upstairs, and almost whooped joyfully when he saw Abel sitting at the table which we used for studying. Abel had a small screwdriver in his hand, and the clock lay face down on the table, with the hour hand and the minute hand beside it. An assortment of little wheels and different parts of the clock were scattered around it. Abel was so engrossed in contemplating the parts of the clock that he did not notice Daddy approaching.

"Nel!" Daddy shouted. "Come up here!"

When Ma went upstairs, Daddy, who stuttered when he was angry or excited, told her, "Y-Y-You a-always s-s-say that I t-t-talk t-that I wanted to s-say t-that something gon happen, b-but t-this time, I d-didn't. T-t-this time I t-tell y-you before. W-w-watch!" And he pointed gleefully at the table, and looked at Abel as if he wanted to hug him.

Ma looked at the dismembered clock with dismay. Then she looked at Abel, who had ceased his contemplation of the clock, and had raised his head to acknowledge the presence of our parents.

Abel's grey eyes focused intensely on Ma and Daddy, before he ventured an explanation. "It was slow, and I was going to fix it."

Ma and Daddy were speechless for a long time before Ma pointed to the assortment of parts on the table. "How you gon fix all of this?" Then, with a sigh of resignation, she began to walk away to prepare dinner. However, she stopped at the head of the stairs, and turned to face Abel. "At least, go and cut a bundle of grass for the cow. The clock done gone," she added, as she walked down the stairs to the kitchen.

Abel left the table, but just before he passed through the door to go downstairs, he stopped at the head of the stairs, turned, and looked wistfully at our radio, sitting on a shelf beside the table.

32 HUMMINGBIRDS AND KARMA by Ram Jagessar

I have a terrible confession. I used to kill and eat hummingbirds.

When I was about 12, my family moved from San Fernando to the Penal area, Mora Dam Road, where my father's cocoa estate was located. I joined the local lads in hunting out and eating anything we could find on the land, and killing whatever wild creatures we found in our path.

There was a huge *jadoo* tree next to my cousin's house, and it swarmed with hummingbirds sampling the flowers for nectar. We young fellers would climb the tree, get close to the birds which had no fear of us, and shoot them with our slingshots.

Then we would roast and eat them, these tiny creatures with bodies small as a single joint of a finger, not even half a bite. I cringe at the memory even now. We didn't need the hummingbirds as food. That was just the way of the *country world*.

And yes, I know there is no forgiveness for my actions, even though I was an innocent boy at the time. I destroyed living creatures who had done me no harm, and Hindu karma says, *I must pay the price in this life or the next*. So, when some little adversity falls on my head, I take it without complaint. I've probably earned it.

I will not talk here about the *iguana, manicou, coscarob*, sardine, *guabin, morocoy* and other creatures I killed and ate, and some like snakes, wasps, centipedes, scorpions, zangys (eels) and frogs we young fellers killed on sight.

Whoops! I forgot the many chickens whose throats I cut, or whose necks I wrung until my father, just before *Ordinary* (O) *Level*[47] exams, told me to stop killing. I did get the top grade in the exam by the sheerest slice of luck, but that must have been for good karma other than stopping the killing of chickens.

---

[47] Equivalent to Grade 12 in North America.

33 THE PUPIL TEACHER by Kennard Ramphal

I was a shy fourteen-year-old when my brother, Andrew, and I passed the Pupil Teachers' Appointment Examination, which qualified us to be hired as pupil teachers. We had attended the Perpetua Kawall Canadian Mission School in the rural district of Canal Number 2 Polder. Our parents were devout Hindus, and we were brought up as Hindus, but nearly all of the schools in Guyana were managed by Christian missionaries, and they hired only teachers who were baptized in their denominations.

Our parents were determined that their children would be successful educationally and told us, "If they want you to be baptized, then baptize, but just remember you will always be a Hindu. No White man gon sprinkle some water on you and make you a Christian."

Andrew was hired as a pupil teacher at Affiance Methodist School on the Essequibo Coast, after he was baptized by the Methodist minister, and I was hired at Wales Canadian Mission School, after being baptized in the Presbyterian Church.

There was no university in Guyana at that time, and only a handful of people who could afford the finances to study at the University of the West Indies or a university in England could earn a degree. No wonder that people who had degrees were well respected in the country. As teachers, we used to say, "If a man has a B.A. (Honors) degree, you have to honor him." This held true, regardless of the area of study.

The structure of the education system in Guyana was quite different from the system in Canada and the United States, where there are boards of education in different areas, with the provincial or state Ministries of Education working with the various boards to coordinate the implementation of education policies. In Guyana, there was a central Ministry of Education, based in Georgetown, with branches in different parts of the country. The Ministry hired inspectors, who visited and evaluated schools in the entire country. Their inspections included the performance of the headmasters or headmistresses and the teachers, and could be a traumatic experience for personnel.

On a fine, sunny Friday morning, Wales Canadian Mission School received a visit from Mr. Sylvester, a school inspector, who had recently returned to Guyana after earning a degree in geology. Why Mr. Sylvester did not seek and obtain employment in his area of expertise remains a mystery to me, but when he darkened the entrance of the main door of our school, we were all nervous, although nobody was unduly worried. The headmaster, Mr. S.I. Das, was an unassuming and kind man, but a stickler for observing the rules established by the Ministry. Our Notes of Lessons were up to date; our weekly education journals, specifying what we had taught for each week, were recorded, and our neat attendance registers were complete for the day, a / for students present, a *0* for students absent.

Mr. Sylvester was a huge man with a booming voice, and his entire manner exuded bluster and confidence. He moved from classroom to classroom as a general would move from troop to troop on the parade square. Eventually, he reached my classroom, where I was teaching an arithmetic lesson in long division. I was quite proud of my prowess in arithmetic and proceeded to teach my lesson confidently, until a hand reached over my shoulder, and I saw a thumb almost as large as the handle of a cricket bat, on the blackboard. I was quite sure that I had written *875* on the blackboard, but when I looked, I saw only *75*. What happened to the *8* I wrote? I asked myself.

"What's this?" Mr. Sylvester asked me in a voice loud enough for the entire class to hear.

I still don't know why I said, "Sorry," but I did, as I replaced the 8 on the blackboard. Mr. Sylvester smirked as he left to inspect another classroom.

After school, at the staff meeting mandated by Mr. Sylvester, the inspector commented on the areas in which the school did well, and the areas in which we needed to improve. "I like the fact that your attendance registers are neat and accurate," he told the staff. "And your Notes of Lessons and Journals are detailed. I like what Mr. Das is doing in this school."

Then he announced in his booming voice, "I saw a pupil teacher make an upside-down eight."

My entire body and mind were on high alert, and my heart raced, because I was quite certain that his announcement was related to his thumb on my blackboard.

Mr. Sylvester looked at me sternly, saw my face mirroring my anxiety, and decided to remove all doubt from my mind, and from the minds of the two other pupil teachers. I shrank in my seat as he pointed to me with his humongous index finger, and pronounced, "Young man, I'm talking about you."

The entire staff was silent, no doubt ruminating on my grievous error, and I felt extreme gratitude to Mr. T.A.J. Singh, the deputy headmaster, a teetotaler and a frank speaker, when he came to my rescue.

Mr. Singh said, "He probably wrote it that way since Standard One, but we all recognize his eight."

Mr. Sylvester was stumped, and frowned as he moved on to other areas of the school. Imagine my relief when the meeting was over.

Afterwards, as I reflected on his comments about my upside-down eight, I wondered whether, on his return to the office of Ministry of Education in Georgetown, and in his report to the Chief Education Officer, did Mr. Sylvester tell him, "One of my biggest accomplishments was that I acquainted the staff that one of the pupil teachers made an upside-down eight?"

The following day, I consulted with the Standard One teacher, Mrs. Persaud, a kind and helpful lady, about the correct way to make an 8, and practiced writing it for a while. In spite of my shyness, I had the utmost confidence in my academic ability, and continued my teaching career with some success.

After I graduated from teachers' college, I joined the Guyana Defence Force as an officer, rose to the rank of captain, and was appointed as the A.D.C. to the President of Guyana. Just before schools closed for the summer holidays, the President hosted a function to recognize the role of the Ministry of Education in promoting the arts in the schools in Guyana, and several education officials were invited.

It was a cool evening, and many of the guests already had quite a few drinks under their belts as they mixed and mingled on the large green lawn of Guyana House, when the band struck the National Anthem, and the President made his appearance, accompanied by yours truly. I moved freely among the guests, chatting and talking about the education of our greatest resource, our children.

Eventually, I joined a group of officials from the Ministry of Education, who were talking animatedly about the renaissance of art in our schools. One man stood out from the others because of his size and his voice, and I instantly recognized Mr. Sylvester, although the bald center of his head was ringed by lush grey hair, and he was slightly stooped. Apparently, he had retained the position of school inspector, and had still neglected to make practical use of his mining degree. He looked at me in my impressive dress uniform. Guyanese had recently freed themselves from the shackles of colonialism, under which all the important positions in Guyana, including the posts of the Governor-General and A.D.C., were held by Whites. People in an independent Guyana were quite proud of the fact that these positions were then filled by Guyanese.

"Young man," Mr. Sylvester smiled as he addressed me. "You look very handsome. We are very proud that people like yourself can be in these positions."

All the rules of etiquette and good manners dictated that I should have simply said, "Thank you! You are very kind." However, my pride in reaching the position that I did in the army, prompted by my huge ego, and the recollection of the humiliation I experienced at the hands of Mr. Sylvester when I was a young pupil teacher, made me neglect the above rules.

Even as I write this, I do not regret the fact that I turned to him, smiled confidently, and told him, "Mr. Sylvester, you may or may not remember me. You visited Wales Canadian Mission School many years ago, and drew the attention of the entire staff on how a pupil teacher made an upside down eight. I was the pupil teacher who made the upside-down eight."

34 LEAVING THE GUARDIAN by Ram Jagessar

In the early eighties of the last century, I worked happily at the *Trinidad Guardian* newspaper. My wife, Jiantee, worked just as happily as a teacher in a secondary school nearby. My sons Arvind, nine years old, and five-year-old Rishi, as far as I remember, were comfortable in a Muslim school, five minutes' walk away. What could go wrong to spoil this rose-coloured life painting?

My job was one of those dream positions that most people never snatch in their lifetimes. I wrote editorials for all three newspapers the *Evening News, Trinidad Guardian*, and *Sunday Guardian*. I could choose my hours, come in and leave when I pleased, as long as I handed in my editorials on time.

I would arrive back at our Curepe home when it was still daylight most days, except Fridays. Sometimes, my two boys and I raced around in the park behind the Muslim school. Or after dinner, we walked to the St Augustine Plaza nearby and sampled ice cream cones filled with coconut, or soursop, or chocolate ice cream. I still remember the taste of that soursop ice cream to this day. Or was it the pleasure of my children's company that made it so delicious?

It was those Fridays that could cause a problem. In addition to writing editorials I reported on the debates in the House of Representatives. Sessions began on Friday afternoon, and sometimes continued until six or seven o'clock. Then I rushed over to the *Guardian* newsroom to write a report on proceedings at the House, and hustle the 10 km. to Curepe, arriving way too late to go to the park, or even take our night walk to the ice cream vendor. But what was one day out of seven to miss the soursop ice cream? I figured the boys would not mind, and it was my job, a dream job in a dream life.

One Friday, I suffered through hours of debate in that tiresome House of Representatives, then spent much time on a lengthy report.

Try reporting on a four-hour parliamentary debate and see how you like it. I arrived home well after eight o'clock, which would be about bedtime for the kids. *No soursop ice cream for you today boys*, I said to myself. I have had my fill of boring irrelevant speeches from the prime minister.

I drove up the slope to my garage under the house, switched off the engine and the lights, and opened the driver side door wearily. It was pitch dark in the garage, and I had to feel my way out to the front steps.

Suddenly I felt something jump up and rest on my leg with no sound. It was Rishi's pet dog, *Patchie*. What the hell is wrong with this stupid dog, I thought. I never touch dogs! And back handed that dog off my leg, a really hard blow.

Now, I was able to see a little. Horror of horrors! It was my son Rishi who had run down the steps to greet me, had held on to my leg because that was as far as he could reach. And I had knocked him down and burst his mouth.

I picked him up from the ground and carried him upstairs. He was silent and hugged me around my neck as if nothing was wrong. He had been waiting patiently for me to come home, and I had knocked him down, and bloodied his lip.

I decided there and then to quit my dream job at the *Guardian*. handed in my resignation and found a teaching job five minutes' walk from home. I would reach home before the boys were dismissed from the Muslim school.

From then on it could be soursop ice cream every day, or maybe even chocolate ice cream for me!

35 DO NOT SPEAK FOR TWO DAYS by Kennard Ramphal

My brother, Balo, twenty years old, and the sixth child of my parents, lived with our parents along with the three unmarried siblings in a sugar-estate housing project at Prospect Village, on the east bank of the Demerara River.

As a graduate from the University of Guyana, Balo was a well-paid teacher, who gave deeper meanings to the words, kindness and unselfishness. Because he was high earning and single, most members of the family, including yours truly, requested financial help from him, which he unhesitatingly granted. His soft voice and endearing manner genuinely came from a pure heart and unblemished mind. Balo. tall, fair and slim, with brown eyes, had dark, black hair, which he kept shoulder length. He had our mother's nose, which curved slightly downward, and was the object of admiration of many young women as he rode his Suzuki motorcycle to and from the high school located about three miles away, where he taught English Language and Literature.

Try as he might, Balo could not get rid of a persistent cold and cough, which he had been battling for over two weeks. He stubbornly refused to see a doctor, in spite of numerous exhortations from our parents, and from his younger siblings.

Our vigorous fifty-seven-year-old father was about five feet, ten inches tall, and the years he spent working in our farm in Canal No. 2 Polder, before we moved to Prospect, had toughened his body. Although he had grown a stomach, his bicep muscles were still firm, and his massive chest strained against his tight shirt. His head was full of grey hair, which he always kept in a crew cut. Daddy, who ruled the house with an iron hand, stuttered whenever he was angry or upset, and everybody, including our mother, a frail soft-spoken woman, who made many sacrifices to maintain a peaceful household, knew to keep quiet whenever he started to stutter.

The walls of our house, like the walls of most houses in Guyana at that time, did not reach up to the ceiling., A space of about three feet between the top of the wall and the ceiling facilitated free air flow in our hot tropical country. This type of construction also allowed sounds to carry across the house.

On the Saturday morning of the third week of Balo's cold and cough, our father was sitting at the kitchen table, eating his breakfast of roti and fried boulangers when he heard Balo's high-pitched cough in the bedroom. "That boy got a cold for over two weeks now, and he don't want to see a doctor. I gon carry him to Dr. Ramroop today," he told my mother.

"I tell him over and over to go and see a doctor and get some medicine for the cold," Ma replied. "I glad you gon take him to the doctor." Ma went and knocked at Balo's door. "Wake up Balo, brush your teeth, and eat something. Your dad gon take you to a doctor for your cold."

"I gon feel better, once I get some more rest," Balo responded, between coughs.

Daddy heard Balo's response, left his breakfast, and joined Ma at the door. "Y-o-o-ou re-e-est l-a-a-ang e-e-enough. And t-t-t-the r-r-rum y-you d-r-r-rink m-m-mek things w-worst," he chastised Balo through the door.

Once he heard the stuttering, Balo jumped out of bed, and came out of his bedroom without further objections. Grabbing his toothbrush from the kitchen shelf, he filled a cup with water, and went to the porch to brush his teeth, while Ma dished out his breakfast. When he entered the kitchen reluctantly, visibly upset at being taken to see a doctor against his will, Ma endeavored to placate him as she placed a plate of roti and boulangers before him.

"You Daddy worried about you," she soothed him. "Remember last month Sugrim had a cold and cough, and he didn't go to see the doctor, and he dead of pneumonia? Go to the doctor and get some medicine for your cold. Besides, you talk in front of all the school children. I don't want you coughing in front of all of them."

None of my siblings would give a harsh response to Ma, with her soft voice and endearing manner, and Balo was no exception. He grunted something which sounded like an assent, and proceeded to eat his breakfast and drink his coffee.

Ma's talk apparently also calmed Daddy, who stopped his stuttering and went in his room to change. Balo and Daddy got a hire car on the East Bank Road, which took them to Stabroek Market. From there, it was a fifteen-minute walk to the doctor's office in Brickdam.

Dr. Ramroop had his consulting office in his *bottom-house*[48]. Almost all of the folding chairs he had set out in the waiting room for patients were filled, and my father and Balo took two of the three vacant chairs, after checking in with the receptionist.

As they prepared for the long wait, my father turned to Balo. "Since we here already, and we got to wait so long, I gon ask Dr. Ramroop about my nose. I gon find out from him why I can't smell. I see three doctors already, and all of them take my money, but can't tell me why I don't smell."

Balo stopped coughing and replied, "It must be a blockage in your nose."

"It can't be a blockage. Remember Dr. Singh charge me fifty dollars to clear the nose, but I still can't smell. I gon ask Dr. Ramroop why. He is a good doctor, and I think that he can tell me why."

Daddy and Balo waited three hours to see Dr. Ramroop, and Balo was a captive audience for Daddy's recounting the history of his smelling woes. At times, Balo didn't really have to cough, but he went into fits of coughing just so that he could get a break from hearing about Daddy's lack of smell and the different remedies he had tried. When the receptionist finally called Balo's name, he was extremely relieved.

---

[48] Loosely describes the ground floor of a house; sometimes open out or with an office in this case.

As soon as Balo and Daddy returned from the doctor, and Daddy opened the door and entered the house, Ma asked anxiously, "What the doctor say? He gave Balo any medicine?"

Daddy put his hands to his lips, pointed to himself, and shook his head from side to side.

Ma was flabbergasted. "Something happened with Balo? Tell me!" Meanwhile the other siblings, Daro, Budhram, and Chano, were mesmerized by Daddy's non-verbal gestures, and were feeling extremely anxious about their elder brother, until Balo walked through the door a few minutes later. He had stopped to make some minor adjustments to his bike parked under the house.

"Balo what happen? You okay?"

"Yes Ma! The doctor gave me some medicine and some tablets. He say I gon be okay."

"Why Daddy doesn't speak?" Daro asked Balo.

"Oh! The doctor told him not to speak for two days," Balo informed them. "Dr. Ramroop told him that he might be able to smell again and may even be able to speak better, but that he must not talk for two days."

For the reader to comprehend why Daddy followed the doctor's instructions to the letter, he must understand the social situation in Guyana, and the role doctors played in the Guyanese society at that time. There were only a few qualified doctors in the country. People who wanted to consult a doctor had to travel to the major cities and wait a long time. Some of them might not be able to see the doctor and would have to return the following day. The few doctors in the country were regarded as minor Gods, and their instructions were followed implicitly.

When Daddy left to visit the latrine, Balo recounted what transpired in the doctor's office. As soon as they went in Dr. Ramroop's office, Daddy started telling the doctor about his nose, and about how he couldn't smell. Then he started telling the doctor about Dr. Singh and the other doctors he saw, and how they couldn't do anything to make him smell again. The doctor told Daddy that the receptionist wrote that Balo Rampersaud was the patient, and asked him if he was Balo Rampersaud.

"No," Daddy replied, "but since I am here, I say that I gon ask you why I can't smell."

"Why did you bring your son?" Dr. Ramroop asked Daddy.

"Oh! He has a cold, but since we here, I want to ask you why I can't smell."

Dr. Ramroop was tired and impatient after seeing so many patients, and thought about the number of patients waiting outside. He put down his pen, faced Daddy squarely, and told him, "From now on, I don't want you to talk for two days." Daddy started to ask for an explanation, but Dr. Ramroop put his right palm outwards to face Daddy. "Heh eh! Not a word for two days." Then he put his index finger on his lips, and repeated, "Two days! Okay? You may be able to smell after you do not talk for two days."

Then he turned to Balo. "Why did you come to see me?"

After Balo told the doctor about his coughing, Dr. Ramroop prescribed some cough medicine and antibiotic tablets, and advised him, "Take these until they are all finished, and the cold and cough should go away. If they don't go away, come back and see me, and I will give you something stronger."

As they got up to leave the office, Dr. Ramroop turned to Daddy, put his index finger to his lips once more, and repeated, "Two days! Remember!"

And that is why Daddy communicated by non-verbal gestures for two whole days.

BOOK TWO

~THE IMMIGRANT EXPERIENCE~

36 CHOOSING A WINTER SPORT by Ram Jagessar

When I reached Canada 23 years ago, everybody tell me I must take up a winter sport.

"This country have long winter and you can't hide in the house for six months," they say. "Take up a winter sport."

I was living in Sudbury, where the people boast they have two seasons, July and winter. So, the question was what winter sport to take? Skating looked nice, but when I watch them skating, I notice a lot of the skaters cutting some sweet high fall on that hard slippery ice. Scratch ice skating.

The next best thing looked to be downhill skiing on one of them nearby slopes right in Sudbury.

My pal, Dan the skiing freak, say, "Boy, you make the right choice. Downhill skiing used to be very dangerous in the old days, but now it really safe."

"How you mean it used to be dangerous?" I ask him.

"Long ago, the ski was hooked on your shoe really solid. So when you fall and slide down the hill, that long ski would hold on to your foot and twist and break your ankle— *pax*! Like a *Crix* biscuit! In those days the ski boot was short, like runners today," Dan explained.

Now he didn't really say, "*Pax* like a *Crix* biscuit," but I felt that it was what he should have said to make it spicy for a Trini.

I had to ask him, "So how they fix that problem?"

"Simple, man," say Dan, already talking like a Trinidadian, "They make the ski boot hard and taller to reach your mid-calf. No more broken ankles. Now your legs break pax! midway between the knee and ankle. Just at the top of the solid boot."

I am sure I hear him say, "*Pax*, this time, and I say, "Not me and downhill skiing."

I decide right away that cross country skiing was the winter sport for me. Good exercise and if you fall you are dropping on soft snow like a foam mattress. I could handle that.

Talking to a neighbour down the street fix my problem of having no skiing equipment. She would lend me her husband's skis, shoes and ski poles that he wasn't using any more. The man had the same size shoes like me, so I had no escape.

I take the equipment from the lady that same evening, and say the next morning I am starting up my winter sport. But looking over the ski poles I notice both of them looked damaged. That lady's husband must have been one doofus of a skier. The metal tip of the ski pole that you had to shove in the snow was bent like a little brushing cutlass instead of being straight like a pin. Easy to fix. I take my hammer and straighten out the tip in the two poles.

Next morning, bright and early, I went up to the beginner's ski trail behind the community college, and put on my equipment. I place my skis in the two grooves like train tracks in the snow and get ready to push off.

Right next to the train tracks I could see some strange round holes in the snow, each one about five inches deep and four inches across. Must be some kind of animal tracks, but I couldn't imagine any wild animal so foolish as to want to go near a college in Sudbury. But no matter. I had my winter sport to start up.

I stand up straight on the skis and give the poles a little push backward. That snow was more slippery than I thought. The skis jumped forward; I fall backward. Trying to balance with my two hands fanning the air, I fall down to one side and my two fists in the gloves make two nice holes in the snow, each one about five inches deep and four inches across. The mystery of the animal tracks was solved.

The animal was me.

I try it a few more times and make more holes in the snow to the left and to the right, and twist some muscles I never know I had.

About the fifth time when I fall, the sole of my right-side ski shoe rip away clean and gone with the ski. Cross country skiing session number one finish early.

Walking back to the car park, I notice some other cross-country guys going to the advanced trail with their ski poles in hand. Something was wrong with all of their ski poles. The tips were all bent like a brushing cutlass—not straight like mine. Then I realize something. The end of them ski poles was supposed to be bent, to dig into the snow better. When I went home, I take my hammer and bend back the ski poles as before, and I never tell the neighbour lady anything about it. I was too shame to be so stupid.

A nice young fellow in the shoe repair shop at the New Sudbury Shopping Centre fixed the damaged shoe, and I went back to try the beginner's trail again, with my properly bent ski poles.

On my first try, I fell first to the right, and then I fell flat on my back, pulling a different set of muscles than the first time. At the fourth try I flopped to the left again, and the sole of the left side shoe just ripped away from the top by about five inches. End of cross-country skiing session two, also early. The neighbour's husband had some rotten shoes but I was more rotten as a cross country skier.

That was the end of my winter sport that year. I figured that if I went out again, something would rip out in me, like my courage. The neighbour came and took back her husband's skiing equipment soon after.

Next winter I got my own equipment and tried cross country skiing by myself again. I made several dozen holes in the snow, pulled a lot of muscles in places I don't care to mention. and let out some blue language on the beginner's trail.

The third winter I gave up and took a beginner's course in cross country. And there the instructor explained that cross country skiing is all about falling down. You are supposed to fall forward when you push the ski poles, but before you actually fall down in the snow your legs come up with the skis and you move forward instead.

Now, how was I expected to know that? The only snow we see in Trinidad was in a snow cone cup with red and yellow syrup and condensed milk on it.

But the instructor was a good man. He showed me how to do my permanent falling down cross-country skiing even in minus 25 weather.

And just as I was getting the hang of it, the whole family move to Toronto. I learn that Toronto don't have anything like winter, and no snow for cross country skiing. If you want to indulge you have to drive way out of town halfway to Sudbury to do cross country. I give away the three sets of cross-country equipment to the Salvation Army.

Later, I learned that it wasn't true there was no cross-country skiing in or near to Toronto. All of the golf courses in and around Toronto converted to cross country skiing trails in winter! By then it was too late to go back to the Salvation Army store to buy back my cross-country skis.

Now, as an experienced Trini-Canadian of thirty winters, I tell you forget about winter sport, forget about winter. Better take up stamp collecting, or minding other people's business, where you are sure to get plenty action.

37 LETTER: RETURN IN FIVE DAYS by Roop Misir

Having come to Canada to pursue higher studies at the University of Manitoba in 1973, my classes ended in April and would resume in September. And with nearly five months to spare, I decided to look for summer employment. However, at that time there was a job scarcity, and international students were allowed to study full-time but were not permitted to look for work and compete with Canadian residents. This meant that all foreign students were required to have the wherewithal to support their studies, i.e., show Canada Immigration proof of secure funds to finance their studies for the upcoming academic year.

To my mind, there had to be a different way to earn some money, not just laze around all summer or do an endless array of summer courses. Or count the rush of cars lining the Pembina Hwy heading to and from the Fort Garry campus of the university. Rather, I came to Canada to get an all-round Canadian education, not merely pieces of parchment, attesting to my degree credentials. In this case, surely some extra money was a big bonus. So, I decided that if I tried hard enough, I should find a job, and must find a job. A real job that anyone, including foreign students would do!

As I found out, jobs were plentiful, but not available to all applicants, including international students and illegal immigrants. Not unexpectedly, summer job preference was given to Canadian citizens, landed immigrants, and in rare cases, to students on visas. However, students on visas must first get permission letters from Canada Employment.

One route I chose to find work was to regularly check Employment Ads posted in the *Winnipeg Free Press*, *The Winnipeg Tribune*, or local community newspapers. Born and raised in colonial British Guiana, English was my first language, and my letter-writing skills were near perfection. So here was an opportunity to show off these skills that would hopefully land me a high-paying summer job.

Every day during the job-hunting period, I spent hours writing three or four applications and addressing and mailing them to different firms in Winnipeg. Of course, I did not forget the typical colonial-style famous ending:

I humbly beg to remain,
Your most obedient servant,
Rupert Misner (Name anglicized)

In the meantime, I got lucky. My landlord's daughter, Marianne, advised me to fill up an application for a job at her workplace, a Tool & Die Co., within walking distance from home. This would be easy—a factory job, and a bit monotonous. Vacancies there were filled mainly by new immigrants.

To get the work permit, I had to go to the Canada Immigration in downtown Winnipeg. At the interview, I provided the immigration officer with the job description and the Job Offer Letter. The interview went so well that the official offered me the written work permit, shook my hand, and welcomed me to the other side of my education—Canadian work experience. He pointed out that my service was in high demand. That I could start work the following Monday.

The wage rate was good—more than twice the daily minimum wage. And since I chose the night shift, I was paid the princely premium of 15 cents an hour. The good thing about this job was that I ended up earning more than enough money to maintain myself for the next year, attend full-time university, pay tuition, and rent, and buy bus fare, plus food, luxuries, beer, and incidentals.

Three weeks later, I received a reply letter from a downtown Winnipeg firm from a previous application. The first thing I saw on the top left-hand corner of the envelope was: *RETURN IN FIVE DAYS*. To say the least, I was so elated that I told my friends of my good fortune. Now I could counsel job hunters on how to get a job—or as I erroneously thought, on how to find another job!

Now if I wished, I could choose to do two jobs and make a lot more money moonlighting for the summer. Was I day dreaming?. However, my friend Ramesh was not so impressed, and what he did tell me served to puncture my inflated ego.

"This is no job offer, man. The words refer to your letter, not you." Then he added, "If the letter is not delivered to the addressee, then it is to be returned to the sender's address."

So my colonial mindset and anglicized names went out of the window!

Times were changing. I felt like a snow cone reduced to a drop of water disappearing on a sizzling pavement on a Winnipeg hot summer day.

38 STOP SMOKING COLD TURKEY by Roop Misir

From my earliest recollections, Pa had always been a cigarette smoker.

On an average day, he would finish a packet of twelve. To cut costs, he chose plain unfiltered cigarettes over the more expensive filter-tipped ones. At times, he'd even roll his cigarettes, using tobacco leaves and rolling paper. As an inveterate smoker, he'd often verbally chastise himself, regretting that he must have his smokes, even while denying myself and his children a penny or two to buy sugar-cake at school. For us, treats were reserved for special days like Christmas and weekends when the local village market comes to life just in front of our house on Martha Street, Windsor Forest, West Coast Demerara (WCD), British Guiana.

Nobody dared question Pa's smoking habit. For brief periods, he voluntarily smoked fewer cigarettes each day. It was his stated desire to kick the habit.

"Baboo, I'd like to quit one day," he often said to me, nonchalantly.

"Good luck, Pa," was my reply.

Not to sell him short, the following week, he happily reported good news: He had stopped smoking altogether!

"Really? How did you do that, Pa? Now consider how much money you'd save every day! Not forgetting the health benefits. For one thing, you'd get rid of that persistent smoker's cough of yours."

"The secret? I boldly took an oath using the Holy Bhagavad Gita. Now I dare not break my oath."

"That's right," I interjected. "The penalty would be far worse than the hazards of smoking."

Fast forward to some twenty years later.

He and Ma came to join us in Saskatoon, Saskatchewan. In the course of our daily conversations, I inquired whether he still read the Gita.

"Of course—yes! Daily readings are part of my routine."

"And what about your smoking?" I asked.

"I smoke now. My oath expired years ago. I am no longer bound by the oath." Then he added, "In Canada, we have far better cigarettes. And they're selling at the giveaway price of only 60 cents for a package of 25. So why shouldn't I smoke? The smokes here are so good that I could go through the whole pack in one blow. Besides, I know economics. That's why I buy by the carton, saving one dollar every time. As for me in my old age, smoking is one of the few pleasures of life." Reluctantly, I nodded.

Finally, I got his message. "As you wish, Pa. Life is made to be enjoyed, but don't go overboard. It's summertime, and it's okay if you smoke, so long as you smoke outside, or in the garage."

For the next few weeks, Pa's health deteriorated. Still, he insisted on smoking. Soon, summer became a distant dream. Autumn came and went. And at the start of winter, Old Man Winter came, and snow enveloped the landscape, six inches thick in our backyard. One day, my father complained about the cold weather. It was so cold that he must dress in winter boots and clothes just to go outside, even in the yard.

"Welcome to Saskatoon weather!" I said.

"Baboo, can I smoke in the house on very cold days? I tried smoking in the garage. It's so cold even though the walls and ceiling are insulated. Is it okay if I smoke in the house?"

"OK, one or two cigarettes only. No more!" I reluctantly agreed.

Pa took this answer to mean that he had the license to smoke at any time and place. And before long he was being his true self, chain-smoking and never looking back. At that time, I decided to warn him that the second-hand smoke was causing breathing difficulties in our three young children. I reminded him to cut out his habit. Alternatively, smoking only outside the house.

"But how come? You smoke in the house, so why the double standard? Baboo, you smoke like a chimney!"

"Only one after meals. That's three at most every day."

"I will stop smoking only if you quit," Pa told me.

I still remember the surprised look on Pa's face when I told him, "Okay I quit. RIGHT NOW! No more smokes!'

As for me, my decision to quit was greeted with a cold post-Christmas advantage. The day was Boxing Day. There were lots of leftovers, not the least being cold turkey pickings. To mark my turning over a new page, I celebrated by imbibing a few stiff drinks. Then after gorging myself with cold roasted turkey, I fell asleep on the basement sofa. When I woke up, late the following day, my persistent smoker's cough vanished like magic in thin air.

That eventful day was four decades ago! I never looked back!

Pa continued smoking, but only when he could do so outside the house. In the warmer months of spring, summer, and autumn, he would revert to his old ways. He later reminded me: *Old habits die hard.*

39 A DOCTOR, AN ACCOUNTANT AND AN ECONOMIST by Kennard Ramphal

My niece, Sarojini, comes from a very prosperous and ambitious family, and each member of the family did everything within his or her power to keep the prestige of the family intact. Nobody was surprised when she married Kumar, an accountant, scion of a wealthy merchant family.

Sarojini and Kumar were well matched. Sarojini was of medium height, slim, and very fair, at a time when fairness was considered an asset because of our British rulers. She was one of the students chosen to attend Bishop's High School, because of her performance at the Common Entrance Examinations. The government had used this examination as the basis for the placement of students in the various secondary schools in the country, and Bishop's High, which admitted only female students, was considered the best. Kumar was a good-looking young man of twenty-five, with thick black hair, which he wore in an Elvis Presley style, and a well-trimmed moustache. He had gone to England to study accounting, and now lived with his prosperous family in a large white house in Camp Street, Georgetown.

When we all immigrated to Canada and found ourselves living in Toronto or its suburbs, we continued to celebrate important occasions together. Sarojini and Kumar did their best to accommodate their hard-drinking—some would say drunken—uncle during parties at their home. Very often, the evening began with a nice quiet dinner, with wine. Then Kumar, and the male invitees, including myself, would progress to scotch and soda. After a few drinks, Kumar went to the kitchen and returned with an aluminum basin, which he placed upside down on his lap, turn to his often-invited brother-in-law, Partab, and say, "Blow a tune, man."

And Partab, in his loud, melodious voice, would burst into song, while Kumar drummed on the basin. I can still remember when I was invited with Partab and a few friends to a party at their place. At about 2:00 a.m., we heard a loud knocking on the door, and when Partab and I opened it, we saw two police officers, one male and one female, on the landing. They seemed bored and slightly angry.

"Would you like a drink of something, officers?" I offered.

"No thanks! We came because your neighbors complained of the noise you are making," the female officer responded. "I realize that you can get carried away after a few drinks, but it's late, and your neighbors want to sleep. Keep it down! Okay?"

"Sorry officers!" Partab told them. "We will stop now."

The police left, after exhorting us not to drink and drive, and the party ended in a somewhat glum note.

Near Christmas of 1984, my niece called me. "I have an important dinner next week Saturday," she announced in a somewhat formal tone. "I am inviting you and auntie, an economist, an accountant, and their wives. It's not a Partab type sport. I know that you are capable of attending a formal dinner. I want you to behave like a doctor." The last sentence referred to the fact that all my relatives were extremely proud of the fact that I had recently graduated with a Ph.D.

"That's quite a dinner, you'll be having."

"Yes," Sarojini replied. "These are important people, and I've been boasting about you."

"What should I wear?"

"You don't have to wear a suit, but dress *good*," she said. Then she added as an afterthought, "None of that sweatpants and hoodie you always wear."

"You got it," I assured her.

On the day of the dinner, I put on my best dress shirt, a red and white sweater in recognition of the season, and a pair of brown trousers. My wife, Leila, wanted to wear her sari, but I assured her that a nice dress would be adequate for the occasion. It was quite cold and windy, and the dusting of snow on the streets was swirling around, as we set out. We had driven to my niece's house many times before, and consequently I experienced no anxiety about my wife finding her way back. We had an unspoken arrangement: I would drive to a party, and she would drive home as the designated driver. I will not insult the reader's intelligence by explaining the reason for this arrangement.

When we knocked on the door of Sarojini house, which was located on Markham Road, north of the 401 Highway, she opened the door to let us in. After I saw her ready to impress in a long dinner dress, a sparkling necklace, and her hair immaculately coiffured and adorned with some sparkling beads, I regretted telling Leila not to wear her sari.

"The economist is already here," Sarojini said. "Come and let me introduce you and auntie."

After putting our coats in the locker, she led me and Leila to the living room to meet the economist, who got up and greeted us enthusiastically. "Dhanraj, I'm so glad to see you. I didn't see you since we met in Guyana. I heard that you were in Canada."

"Ramlall, how are you doing? I, too, heard that you were in Canada, but I didn't know how to contact you. How did you know my niece?"

"She was in one of my classes at the University of Guyana when I was lecturing there."

Before I left the university to join the Guyana Defence Force, Ramlall and I were in the same class in the University of Guyana, and had some memorable drinking bouts together. We started reminiscing about Guyana and about the university, until we were interrupted by the doorbell.

"That's the accountant," Sarojini observed as she gathered her dress and went towards the door.

After hanging up the coats of the accountant and his wife, she ushered them into the living room, and started to make the introductions, but was surprised when he nudged her aside. "Dhanraj," he shouted. "Man, I haven't seen you since you left Wales School to join the Guyana Defence Force. Everybody said that you forgot all about us."

"Nah, man. I was just busy. Nice to see you again, Gobin. How you know Sarojini?"

"Through her husband," he replied. "We studied in England together."

"Those were nice times we had at the junior staff club," I reminded Gobin. "I didn't even know how to hold a billiard cue until you guys showed me. Now, I'm not such a bad player. Except when I have too much to drink," I added.

Although his next remark was addressed to me, Gobin turned to the others in the living room, and laughing loudly, remarked, "I remember when you passed out leaning against the pool table."

The evening commenced with very fine wine, poured in crystal glasses. As we sipped our wine, Kumar, Gobin, Ramlall and I looked at each other, each one of us knowing that the others were thinking that scotch would be better, but restraining ourselves because Sarojini worked so hard to prepare for a sophisticated occasion. When Sarojini indicated that it was time for dinner, and led the way to the dining table, I was astonished by the sparkling display. The silver cutlery was polished to a shine, and there were two crystal glasses per person, one for water and one for wine. Blue embroidered napkins were neatly folded and placed beside the plates, but there were no plates.

When I looked quizzically at Sarojini, she whispered to me, "We will be served."

Sarojini went to one end of the table, while Kumar sat at the other end. "You sit at my right, and auntie will sit beside you," she told me.

Then she assigned places to everyone, ensuring that Gobin would sit next to Kumar, so that they could reminisce about their experiences in England, while the lady hired by Sarojini to help and serve for the evening stood by the kitchen. When Sarojini indicated that we were ready to be served, the lady brought in the first course.

The cream of mushroom soup was served in deep China soup bowls, followed by a delicious salad. For the main course, we were served choice cuts of beef in Sarojini's best China. Dessert was the best part: custard, followed by Gulab-jamun, in a sweet syrup.

Sarojini had no need to showcase me to her guests, because they both knew me, but throughout dinner, she emphasized my role in the army, my stint as ADC to the President of Guyana, and of course my recently acquired Ph.D., as we all helped ourselves to the rich red wine.

After dinner, the male guests retreated to the living room, and Sarojini and the women went upstairs to the game room to talk about whatever women talk about in these situations. We were allowed to take our wine glasses to the living room.

"This wine is good," Gobin said, "but I can still feel the chill from the wind in my bones."

Kumar took the hint immediately. "You want something stronger?"

Although the question was addressed to Gobin, Ramlall and I answered in unison, "Yes! Scotch would be good."

Kumar extracted a forty-ounce bottle of Chivas Regal from the liquor cabinet and placed it on the coffee table.

"I'll go get glasses," he told us, as he left for the kitchen. In a few moments, he returned with four crystal glasses. "You guys will chase with water or soda?"

"Soda!" we all replied.

We set aside our wine glasses, poured liberal amounts of scotch, and savored the drink as it burned its way down our throats. The first one was followed by a few more.

Then Kumar turned to me and uttered his famous inebriated words, "Blow a tune, man," as he left for the kitchen.

I needed no prompting. As soon as Kumar returned with an aluminum basin, I burst into a song which I had sung many times in my drinking bouts. Kumar kept the rhythm on the basin, and the others clapped.

I sang, "Gal from Polder, come doh doh pon me shoulder. Tea cup and saucer, to give me loving water."

Whether he was inspired by my singing, or whether he felt that he could do better, Gobin volunteered to sing the next song, followed by Ramlall. As I clapped to keep time for Ramlall's song, I saw my niece walk down the stairs and look upon the group with displeasure, before she scowled and returned upstairs to join the ladies. Being fortified with good scotch—we were into our second bottle by this time—we ignored Sarojini and continued with our loud songs and drumming. None of us heard the knocking at the door, and we were surprised when we saw Sarojini answer the door.

"You all gon stop this noise, or you want me to call the police again?" The voice was loud and insistent.

"That's my neighbor," Kumar explained.

At the door, we saw a man with a long beard, a dressing gown over his pajamas, and a black coat over it all. A grey tuque was thrown carelessly over his head, and specks of snow were all over his outer clothing. He kept dusting the snow from his coat as he spoke.

"I'll speak to the men," Sarojini told him, placatingly.

"I'm surprised that the walls of this house aren't thick enough to keep out the noise," Gobin offered by way of explanation. Then he decided to throw a sop to Cerberus. "You want a drink?" he asked the neighbor.

"I want you to keep your noise down so that I can sleep," the neighbor snarled, as he turned away to return to his house.

As she closed the door, Sarojini looked at Kumar, then at me, and finally thew a scorching glance at Gobin and Ramlall. She was about to address the group when she was interrupted by Leila, who spoke directly to me, "Dhanraj, you guys made enough noise. It's time for us to go home."

Quite contrite, I meekly nodded. As we put our coats on, and just before we walked out the door, Sarojini came up, and told me in a scathing tone, "I invited a doctor, an economist, and an accountant to a formal dinner. And look what happened!"

For a few moments, guilt rendered me speechless. Then emboldened by the immense amount of alcohol I had consumed, I muttered, "You invited people, not titles," before I allowed Leila to lead me to our car.

Just as we walked through the door, I heard Sarojini mutter to herself, "You can take them out of Guyana, but you can't take Guyana out of them."

It's been over thirty years since that memorable occasion, and I was invited to my niece's house many times after this incident, but never to a formal dinner.

40 THE MIGRATION GAME by Ram Jagessar

August 1993

Trinidadians who find their lives boring and weary can now take advantage of my experience, gained right here in Sudbury in Canada. Migrate, I say, and be bored no more. You may find yourself frustrated, bewildered, unemployed, and suddenly appreciative of idiot relatives. But I say again, bored you will not be.

To make things a little more interesting, choose a country that is the very opposite in size to yours. Try one with a strange culture and people who are nothing like you at all. And make your move when the climate of the new country is at its worst. If you are a sucker for punishment, pick a country with a different language.

Migration is exactly what my family and I did three winters ago, making what I call a 30-30 switch. We jumped from the little South Caribbean Island of Trinidad, steaming at 30° Celsius, straight into a Sudbury snowstorm at -30°.

Coming up from Toronto, my elder son was so excited at his first glimpse of snow that he got out of the car and ran about to catch the snowflakes on his tongue. I notice that he's not so keen now when he has to go out and catch them on a snow shovel.

My smaller boy was worn out just by the six-hour night trip down Highway 400 and Highway 69. While we dodged maniacal tractor trailers, homicidal rock cuts and peered through blinding snow, he fell fast asleep. The streets of Sudbury were paved neither with gold nor silver, but with dirty ice, and salty snow. Some streets didn't seem to be paved at all.

That night I looked around for a mango tree to put my lighted *deya*[49]. None could be found. My sister's yard had several pine trees

---

[49] Small clay pot used in the Hindu Festival Of Lights

in her yard. I picked one out and put the deya at its base. Next morning when I checked, the oil in the deya had frozen solid and the light had gone out, probably minutes after I placed it down.

Sudburians in thick parkas walked their dogs along the snow tunnels posing as sidewalks. They carefully looked the other way while their pets added to the piles of frozen doggie doo-doo to be thawed in April. No pet owner walked with his pooper-scooper. And you call this a civilized country!

Settling down here could be described as stimulating, when it wasn't terrifying. For example, you were walking on snow and ice for the first time, with four Woolco bags in each hand, when you saw a pair of boots fly up in front your face. As the ground jumped up and hit you in the back of the head, you realized those were your boots. You got your first major winter wipeout and went sprawling in the snow, your wallet conveniently falling in a half-frozen puddle. Something to write home about.

I remember well the first time I drove from New Sudbury to Civic Square to get my OHIP[50] number. I was driving for the first time on snow and ice, in a strange car, and on the right-hand side instead of the left. Plus, I had no experience driving an automatic car, especially one with the rear window defogger not working. And of course, I didn't know any of the streets, and had to keep one eye on the map, one eye on the road ahead, one eye looking for street signs not covered with snow, and one eye looking up for divine guidance.

Then I reached Civic Square and found there was no place to park. I parked the car in the first empty space I saw, which was in front of Golden Grain bakery, and headed off to the OHIP office.

When I was finished with OHIP, I couldn't remember the entrance I used to go into Civic Square. I couldn't remember the place where I parked the car. In fact, I couldn't recollect the make, model or registration number of the miserable vehicle.

I considered asking for help. Excuse me, sir, but I cannot find my car. I know it's a red car. I have the key, but I can't remember

---

[50] Ontario Health Insurance Plan

anything else about it except that the rear window defogger is not working. Could you help?

Not a good idea! I walked round and around Civic Square until I came across my car parked up on the curb in front of Golden Grain bakery. It didn't have a ticket on it. And it started too.

Sudbury was a little bit strange. Every person, street, house, car, fire hydrant and dog I saw in Sudbury was strange. For a long time, I did not bother to look into people's eyes. What's the point, since I didn't recognize anybody. I stood out like a penguin in a pig farm. Nobody in the supermarket or the bank had brown skin. Nobody had black hair; it was all blonde, brown, red, sandy or receding. This is not a joke—at first a lot of White people looked the same.

Everything was new. I was a child again. I had to learn a zillion things all at once, like how to dress for the cold, how to drive, how to walk on ice. I had to find out where to buy clothes and food, where the offices were, and where to locate people like mechanics and dentists, and most important, the washrooms. When you move into a cold climate your bladder goes into fast forward mode.

Other Sudburians talked about things I didn't understand. They got excited about that immensely dull game of hockey, and some geek named Gretzky. On television all I could see was a bunch of bruisers in padded outfits swatting at an invisible object, when they took time from punching each other out. Sports pages were full of weird stuff like curling. To this day I have no idea what ringette is.

I never did any skating, snowmobiling, bowling, bingo or ice fishing. Nor am I bilingual. Maybe it was a good thing I was not a *one of the crowd type*. I forgot to mention that I am a vegetarian, do not smoke, gamble, curse, drink beer, coffee or hot drinks generally, and I have never liked Elvis. So I didn't fit in easy.

But I am still here. Canada is a good place to live, and Sudbury is one of the better spots. I am over forty, and also a father of two. I'm born again, in a non-religious way. I hope I don't have to move to Manitoba. You can overdo this born-again business.

41 SWIMMING OBSESSION by Roop Misir

The sign at the Winnipeg International Airport read, *Welcome to Friendly Manitoba*. I was thrilled to arrive in Winnipeg.

A very good friend, Ramesh received me and took me to stay at his apartment on Sherbrook Street. He helped me to successfully adjust to the new human ecosystem. Everything was fine and I was settling well, except for one obsession. I missed my swimming!

Before coming to study in Canada at the University of Manitoba—Winnipeg, I wondered whether I would be able to continue my swimming hobby in Canada. I would have to be looking for a place to swim.

But, Boy, O Boy! Could I find a place similar to my favorite Swimming Bridge in Windsor Forest, West Coast Demerara, Guyana, my mecca swimming bath? As it turned out, that wasn't meant to be!

As a tropical country just north of the equator, Guyana enjoys 20-35°C year-round. In contrast, the Canadian weather changes in the four seasons. The current September weather temperature was around 10°C, dropping further in the winter months to the extreme low, down to -40°C in February. As for my favorite obsession, the reality was that swimming must be done indoors, in dedicated swimming pools encased in metal and glass. To say the least, I wasn't too thrilled with this!

Finally, reality did step in. I was forced to conclude that when in Winnipeg, do what the people do. In this case, swimming indoors during the cold months. And with some luck, I would hope to do a month or two of outdoor swimming in the summer.

COMPROMISE

My new friend, Fred, informed me that he worked out and swam at the University of Manitoba Phys Ed Gymnasium on most days. So, I asked him if I could accompany him.

"No problem," replied Fred. "You can come with me. I plan to go during the lunch period next Wednesday. I'd be happy to show you around. And if you like what you see, then you can go every day, or once or twice a week. It's that simple." Then Fred continued, "There's no charge. Your student card entitles you to use the gym facilities. Is this okay with you?"

"Sure!"

On the appointed day, Fred gave me a grand tour of the Men's Gym. It was ultra-modern, practical, and very user-friendly. However, one practice did stand out—nude men walking with their private parts dangling. What a site to behold! To say the least, I was surprised beyond words.

In my country Guyana, our upbringing was a bit different. Paramount was a person's right to privacy—whether at home, outside the house, or in public spaces. We were not accustomed to exposing our private body parts in public. This nudity exposure was a sudden surprise. It came as a culture shock. There and then, I decided against joining the men's gym!

TRADE-OFFS

I realized that I was privileged to attend a top-class University in Canada. As for my love for swimming, I knew that I had to make compromises: I would have to learn to live with what was available. Or be creative. My favorite all-weather Swimming Bridge in Guyana was no longer an option, but only a fond memory.

To be realistic, I had to find alternatives, but in the meantime, I put *public/pubic* swimming on hold.

"No," to the men's gym. "Yes," to bathtub and shower.

No big deal. I could live with that!

42 BREAKING PLATE GLASS by Roop Misir

After years of study in the academic world, plus animal science research at the University of Alberta, my Ph.D. dissertation was complete and ready to be submitted—a watershed moment for me. The night before, I barely had an hour of sleep. My mind was operating on overdrive.

The privilege to study at such a prestigious Canadian university, coupled with earning the degree in only three years was no mean accomplishment. They represented the twin badge of excellence. I spent three months writing, reading, and proofreading the manuscript. To graduate with the spring convocation batch, I was required to submit three copies of the bound thesis to the Office of the Faculty of Graduate Studies. A few days before, I had already received an offer of a research position at the University of Saskatchewan, Saskatoon. The submission deadline for my completed thesis was noon, February 24, 1982.

I was apprehensive. Just before leaving my Animal Science office at 9:30 a.m., I met with the office administrative staff, proudly telling them that finally, my hard work was coming to a favorable end. With their good wishes, I left with copies of my bound thesis in hand for the two-minute walk to the Graduate School Office.

The weather was fine and the path clear—not too cold for a midwinter day. A plethora of thoughts kept my mind in a state of dynamic equilibrium. Then a few questions popped out mentally, complete with answers:

Who am I? *Roopnaraine Misir.*

How do I know that I am?

Cogito ergo sum! I think therefore I am!

So many years of academic pursuit made many things seem so very easy to me. Before I knew it, I was nearing the door of the

Graduate School Office. Still, in deep thought, I was heading for my destination. As I extended my hand to open the door by pulling at the knob, the tips of three of my fingers touched the glass instead. Instantly, the sound of cracking shatterproof glass filled the air. And not surprisingly, I walked straight through the door!

For a moment, I was embarrassed and unable to think rationally. A crowd of office staff quickly gathered around, the Vice-Chancellor and Vice-Principal among them.

How did this happen? I asked myself.

The V.P. said, "Are you okay? Are you hurt? Do you need to go to the University hospital across campus?"

"No Sir! I am fine, not a scratch, not a scrape." Then I thought about the broken glass, and asked him, "How much do I have to pay for walking into the glass?"

"Nothing. It was an unfortunate accident," he replied.

After I explained what happened, the V.C. congratulated me, hugged me, and wished me all the best!

Then I looked back at what had happened. The door was still standing, but something very unusual stood out. The shattered glass had the outline of a human figure. It was so real, enigmatic as if hand-carved or sculpted by an artist! Many people commented on the incident. However, one remark stuck with me to this day: "I've never seen anything like this. It's surreal," one lady observed.

In the corporate world, we often hear the oft-repeated expression, *Breaking the glass ceiling*, as a reference to the metaphor for the invisible barrier that prevents some people from rising to senior positions. In contrast, I broke a thick, one-inch plate glass of the door to academia.

What does this portend? Take it as you wish!

In retrospect, as the son of a rice farmer happily earning money helping to feed the nation in faraway Guyana, little did I ever in my wildest dreams expect to achieve the highest academic degree at a prestigious university!

43 I'LL RAISE MY PRICE by Kennard Ramphal

My wife and I were removing the fifteen-year-old beige carpet in the upper storey in our house, and replacing it with an oak floor, and we had to sleep in the family room in our basement for a while.

As I dressed the following morning—a Thursday, the disruption and the change in routine caused me to forget my wallet, containing my driving license, my credit cards, and some spending money. Luckily, I remembered my employee pass and the office key, which were on a chain around my neck.

At that time, I was teaching co-op education in the Scarborough Centre for Alternative Studies (SCAS). The school was located in a building physically attached to Centennial College, although SCAS was operating under the auspices of the Toronto District School Board. A long corridor connected SCAS with Centennial, and the staff and students at SCAS used the corridor to access the food court at Centennial.

Before classes started, I decided to grab a coffee from the Tim Hortons outlet in the food court. I had the habit of having my money in my hand before I reached the counter in order to save time, and I frowned at people who ordered coffee, and took what seemed like hours to search their pockets or purses for money. When I reached into my pocket for my wallet, my hands came out empty, and as I turned away, I thanked God that I did not embarrass myself by ordering a coffee, and then discovering that I had forgotten my wallet.

I prided myself on my popularity at SCAS, and thought that it would be no problem to borrow some money from one of my colleagues. My first mark was a teacher of English, Kim Wilson, with whom I was always bantering.

"Kim, I forgot my wallet at home this morning. Can you lend me ten dollars until tomorrow?" I asked the slim, tall blonde.

"The last person I lent money to quarreled with me when I asked her to repay the money, and I promised myself that I will not lend money to anyone again," she responded in a no-nonsense tone.

"You should have said *The last person to whom I lent money*, not *the last person I lent money to*," I told her sullenly, as I retreated, and considered whom I should target next.

Then I thought of Ram, a teacher from Trinidad, who was sitting at his desk, grading students' assignments. When he looked up as I approached, I noticed that his eyes were bloodshot, and I knew that he had been drinking the previous night. Most teachers suspected that he had a problem with alcohol, but nobody voiced a concern.

"Ram, I am doing renovations in my home, and I forgot my wallet," I told him. "Can you lend me ten dollars for coffee. I will pay you back tomorrow."

It seemed to me as if Ram's eyes became a few shades redder as he opened the drawer of his desk, took out two packets of Nescafe instant coffee, and offered them to me. "The kitchen has a kettle, and the fridge has milk and sugar. You can heat water and make a coffee," he told me, as he re-focused on grading the assignments.

"No thank you, Ram," I responded as I walked away, disappointed.

Walking back to my office, I rationalized, I can't really blame him. So many people in the streets asked me for a looney to buy a coffee, but I knew that they were going to buy cheap wine with the money they collect.

I resolved not to embarrass myself further and ask anybody else for a loan until I approached my office and saw Pat, with whom I co-taught co-op, sitting in her office. Pat was hired at SCAS as a hair-dressing teacher initially, but switched to co-op after she discovered that she had developed allergies to certain hair dressing products. She was slim, of medium height and with a beautiful face which always wore a smile. She had the bluest eyes I ever saw, but I could not determine the color of her hair, because she changed the color monthly, each color complementing her natural beauty. I should have asked her in the first place, I thought.

I pushed my head inside her office. "Pat, I am doing some renovations to my home, and in the confusion, I forgot my wallet. Can you lend me ten dollars until tomorrow?"

"Sure, Ken!" She opened her bag, fished out a ten-dollar bill, and handed it to me.

"I promise to repay it tomorrow," I told her holding my right palm shoulder high, as I pocketed the ten dollars.

By then, my longing for a coffee fix had evaporated, but the ten dollars in my pocket gave me a sense of security. In the afternoon, although I did not badly need a coffee, I went to Tim Hortons, and treated myself to a café mocha and a honey cruller doughnut, just because I had the money to pay for it. As I enjoyed them, I promised myself that I would not forget my wallet the following day.

Pat and I were scheduled to monitor some students who were doing their co-op placements in the Multicultural Community Interpreter Services, MCIS for short, at 12:00 noon on the next day. As I pulled into the parking lot, I was pleasantly surprised to see an ex-soldier of the Guyana Defence Force, Ami John, who served in the platoon I had commanded. He was now the parking lot attendant. We had a pleasant chat before I went in the office to meet with the students and their supervisors. Pat came later to join me in the office.

We often treated the supervisors of our co-op students to lunch as a token of our appreciation for hosting the students. In this case, the supervisor, a vivacious lady of about forty, decided to meet us at a restaurant located about fifteen minutes away, and Pat and I decided that it would be better to go with my car. I still remember the curious look on Ami John's face as I escorted Pat to my car.

When we returned from lunch, I suddenly remembered the ten dollars that I had borrowed. I knew that I was very forgetful, and was determined to repay my debt before it slipped me.

"Pat, I owe you ten dollars. I better repay you now," I told her, as I reached for my wallet.

"Not here! Not now!" she almost screamed.

"But if I don't give you the money now, I will forget," I insisted.

"Not here! Not now!" Pat repeated, waving her arms frantically.

I happened to glance at Ami John whose mouth was open and whose eyes were almost out of their sockets, but I kept on insisting that Pat take the money I owed her. By then two other people in the parking lot had their eyes on us, and Pat, who obviously didn't want to prolong the scene, reluctantly accepted the ten dollars.

On my way out of the lot, at the end of the day, I handed Ami John five dollars along with the parking ticket.

"Ten dollars!" he said.

"But the sign says five dollars for the whole day."

"Five dollars for parking. But whatever that gorgeous lady did must have been worth more than ten dollars. With all due respect, Captain, I didn't know that you were so cheap."

I handed over five dollars to Ami John, and decided to leave him to ponder the mystery. Driving on the 401 on my return to SCAS, I realized why Pat made such a fuss about accepting her own money, and knew that I owed her an apology.

Back at school, I popped my head in her office. "I now realize why you didn't want to take the ten dollars in the parking lot. That ex-soldier was surprised that you charged me only ten dollars."

Pat flashed her blue eyes at me, grinned wickedly, and told me, "I'll raise my price."

44 NO NEED TO SCRATCH YOUR HEAD by Ram Jagessar

When you live in Canada you get all kinds of free offers in the mail. And if you are like me, a new arrival, you don't know which ones are good, and which ones are too good to be true.

When I was living in Sudbury, my mailbox yielded a scratch card that looked very promising. "Scratch the hidden number boxes. and you may well have a chance to win a valuable prize," it said. It was free. Nothing to lose, no money to send. So I scratched and found myself a winner!

"If you win, call this number," was the instruction, and so said, so done.

A voice on the other end confirmed I had indeed won a prize which would be delivered to my house if I agreed to listen to a short presentation with my spouse. The voice was most insistent that spouse had to be on hand. Neither the prize nor the presentation was specified. Nothing to lose, and a prize to gain. It looked like a win-win. I agreed.

A nice young fellow in a suit turned up with a huge suitcase and a briefing binder from which he started reading to me and my wife. Obviously, he hadn't memorized it yet. Sounded like a junior salesman coming up against an old hardcase like me.

"Isn't your health the most important thing in your life?" He looked at me and spouse. We looked at each other and nodded.

"Research has shown that polluted air and dust are among the major reasons for ill health." My wife and I agreed that it was so. "Wouldn't you welcome a health system that cleaned the air and removed harmful dust from your house?"

Spouse and I would certainly consider such a system. How much would it cost? Nice young fellow ignored that and proceeded to unpack his big suitcase and unveil a machine that looked very much like a vacuum cleaner.

"Isn't that a vacuum cleaner? We have a perfectly good vacuum cleaner, you know!" my wife said.

"No, no, this is your new health system," the young fellow responded quickly. "This machine doesn't spill out dusty air from the back, but cleans and perfumes the air. Any dust picked up is captured in a separate water container, which can be emptied after use. This machine mops the floor, scents the house, and also picks up the slightest dirt and dust."

"So, it is a vacuum cleaner after all?"

"Much more than a vacuum cleaner," the young fellow insisted. "It is the most powerful vacuum cleaner on the market. It will clear out any trace of bad stuff from recognized dust traps like carpets. It will pick up a sixteen-pound bowling ball, so strong is the suction."

He plugged in the health machine, threw out a mixture of sand, corn flakes and little steel balls on my carpet and his machine swallowed it in seconds, leaving the carpet gleaming clean. "Voila!"

Seeing some hesitation still on our faces, because he hadn't told us the price yet, young fellow launched his *coup de grace*. "Do you have a vacuum cleaner?"

"Yes," my wife and I exclaimed.

We brought out the vacuum, bought about six months before, and he asked me to vacuum an area of the carpet.

"Did you think you have vacuumed out all of the dust?"

"Of course," I replied. "This is a good machine."

The young fellow would show that my vacuum was no good, a piece of junk. He opened his health machine and put a white filter over his health machine hose, so we could see the results for ourselves. Then took his machine and vacuumed the same spot I had vacuumed with my old, useless machine. Then, he pulled out the house hose, and showed us a visible layer of dust on the filter!

"What do you say now? Doesn't it show how superior my health machine is to your obsolete vacuum cleaner?"

My wife and I showed on our faces that it could be true. Now, he answered our question about the cost of the health machine, and finally told us that the price for his machine was $2400.

I nearly had a heart attack, but he parried my shock with an offer of $500 for my old vacuum, a princely offer for something which I had bought for $200. I would actually be getting $300 on the deal! Now I would get the health machine prize for only $1900!

I countered with a confession we did not have that kind of money on hand, and he riposted that he had convenient payment plans! I declined his payment plan and laid down the final word that we were not taking his health machine.

Very confused and angry when I turned him down flat, young fellow flung the cheap gift at me, which I estimated would cost about $2 in Walmart, packed up his trash, and stormed out.

I figured he was losing his commission of about $500—not bad for two hours of work. His machine could not cost more than $300 to manufacture, a further $200 to sell to young fellow's company. They would have cleaned up $1400 on that one sale!

The young fellow had a good pitch but he had never met a hard case like me. I knew part of the plan was to buy my vacuum and take it away, so I couldn't compare with his machine if I bought it.

In addition, I knew his master stroke of showing his machine would get dust from a carpet after mine had cleaned, was a scam. No machine, however powerful, picks up all the dust from a carpet. If I had done the filter trick on my vacuum and cleaned a carpet *after* his health machine, I would get the same circle of dust. That was why he wanted to buy my vacuum for that ridiculous price, to get it away from my house.

My spouse and I had a good laugh at this unscrupulous young rogue who was ripping off ignorant homeowners left and right.

After that, we never scratched any more scratch cards in the mail. Now when I get any mail or email which starts with, "You have won!" I delete it instantly, or throw it in the garbage.

45 KEEPING WATCH ON CHRISTMAS DAY by Roop Misir

Raj and Naresh, new immigrants to Canada, were lifelong friends.

Initially, both did odd jobs in Toronto, until they chose to work as security guards. At that time there was a construction boom, and jobs were plentiful and rewarding. Often, they could choose to work many job site shifts. With new mega-projects starting regularly, the city skyline was dotted with numerous construction cranes—a good indicator of progress and economic growth.

Before coming to Canada, both were qualified in their fields However, they chose the security guard route because the job was easy, and the pay could be quite lucrative. Besides, there was always the option of overtime work, further fattening their weekly pay cheques.

Both were married, with families. Also, both would have loved to upgrade their education on a full-time basis; however, they couldn't afford to study full-time. Instead, they did part-time diploma courses, while working full-time to provide for their respective families.

GUYANESE CHRISTMAS

Back in the old country of Guyana, Christmas Day was a national holiday, celebrated by people from all religious backgrounds. In Toronto, the two friends remembered with great fondness the back-home festivities of the season. They had to find a way to enjoy this grand occasion, even while reporting for duties on Christmas Day.

Both men accepted the challenge and reported for work. They loved the triple holiday pay, so they signed up for many shift openings, occasioned by fellow security guards taking the day off. So, they devised a clever strategy. Each would work as many as three different sites concurrently. In doing so, they were ignoring the rule that management allowed only one person to one job site, and not at three concurrent job sites.

NO SECURITY CAMERAS

Those were the days when worksites had no security cameras, no computers to record worksite timetables, and no cell phones. Securing three sites did however require some creative thinking and an innovative approach. Since the three sites were within a five-minute commuting time by car, each guard would clock in at their first site, then phone the guards at their other two sites to clock them in, claiming they would be a few minutes late, being held up in traffic due to the unusually heavy snowfall the night before.

Sounds reasonable? Yes!

As it turned out, they had both succeeded in getting their timecards checked in. After checking at the first site, they stayed for five to ten minutes, then continued the rounds, and visited each site once or twice every hour. So far so good!

BRILLIANT IDEA

Then Raj came up with what seemed to be another brilliant idea. "Let's go home and observe the Christmas festivities."

Observe, meant to take it easy, no more than one or two drinks. Get in the holiday spirit, not to get high. In contrast, to celebrate, meant going flat out and having drinks unlimited!

"So, what's next?" Naresh said.

"Each of us can manage the three worksites from home. We can leave home to visit the work occasionally."

Naresh exclaimed, "A piece of cake. Real Christmas Cake!".

So, they gave it a try. And as they expected, this new formula worked very well, until after lunch. Suddenly the shift supervisor,

Jack, was making spot checks. He looked and checked, but still no signs of either Raj or Naresh at their registered worksites. Both men were absent from all six sites. In desperation, Jack decided to phone Naresh at his house.

"Naresh," he said hurriedly. "Where are you? Aren't you supposed to be at one job site, or at all three sites? I checked all the logbooks. You …You signed up for THREE, but now you are present at NONE of the sites!"

"Not to worry, Sir. We can explain," he answered nonchalantly. "I am aware that many of our guards are off today, so I thought I was doing the company a favor by securing three sites. I moved from site to site in my car. Yes, MY CAR!" he stressed. "I was doing the company a favor by keeping all the sites secure."

The boss was surprised, if not angered:

"I will file a complaint against you for dereliction of duty."

"And what does that mean?" Naresh retorted barefacedly.

"I'll explain when I meet you." Then the supervisor continued, "You just tell me. Where the hell are you? I must see you on the job right NOW."

Of course, Naresh was at home. But since he was living not far away from the coffee shop, he said: "I am McDonald's having a coffee— Christmas special java-jive coffee!"

In the spirit of the season, Jack accepted the explanation and agreed to join both men for coffee at McDonald's. A merry atmosphere of Christmas pervaded the air. For a few hours at least, the infectious spirit of Christmas transformed the guards and the supervisor into happy winners.

As Guyanese say: Happy Christmas and a Prosperous New Year.

The illustrious Bard Shakespeare put it. *All's well that ends well.*

46 LOST AT DISNEYLAND by Roop Misir

After a long and eventful day enjoying the magic of Disneyland, we were tired, and decided to head for the car. I had parked it in the large 120-acre lot designed especially for fans and attendees of the Walt Disney Wonderland, Orlando, FL. The year was 1982.

It was past midnight, but with so many wonderful things to see along the way en-route to the car, by the time we reached the monorail to take us to our parking lot, it was about 2:30 a.m. So, what to do? Sure, we wanted to get the car. But where was the car?

That was the million-dollar question!

You see, in the places where I've lived over the years, the parking situation was different. Normally, I would park in the yard, in the garage, or at times on the roadside curb. There was no problem finding the car whenever I needed it. In small paid lots, the concierge would give patrons a ticket upon entry, to be paid when exiting the lot. So, there was never a problem retrieving the vehicle.

This time though, the parking system was different. Very different! For one thing, the Disneyland parking lot was sprawling and had a multitude of attractions. Or rather a plethora of pleasant and distracting activities. As well as its novelty, a monorail system moved passengers in one direction only from the Parking Lot to the center of the attractions; another took fun-filled patrons back to the Parking lot at the end of the day's visit.

At the Wonderful World of Disney, life centered around magical cartoon characters, like Mickey Mouse, Minnie Mouse, Daffy Duck, etc. Having fun and escaping reality was a new adventure every day.

I knew the car license plate number, numbers for the parking space, and the lane numbers. However, what I hadn't done at the time we boarded the trains, was to note the name of the starting station where we boarded. Unfortunately for me, I became aware of this requirement after it was too late!

Now as we were finding our way to my car, I was lost for words and directions to find the car.

I was desperate; the members of my party were getting increasingly confused.

My wife, Ramdai, and four young children placed implicit faith in me, and I felt terrible for letting them down. I was the father figure to whom they looked up. Of course, no one complained. Everyone was tired and sleepy. However, this did not deter me from being embarrassed and ashamed. Still, I took a few deep breaths to reduce anxiety and feelings of guilt. Also, in the event I had to do some explaining later, I was mentally preparing a list of questions and answers as to why and how at times things could go wrong.

Amid the confusion, we sometimes curse and swear. But more often we remember that perhaps we should seek divine guidance. Such help, like a blessing, is free. There's no harm in trying. And results can be immediate and miraculous, or a test of endurance. So, let's do what we have to do, take a number and wait your turn.

So, when I made my mental plea, instinctively, the words "God help us," burst forth from my parched lips. Then to my surprise, I heard our little daughter, Renuka, who had earlier lost her Mickey Mouse toy, crying, "I want my Mickey Mouse." And the lightbulb in my head lit up!

Surely, when in need there's Divine help. To me, God's message was that the car was within range. A long shot, but as they say, a drowning man clutches at a straw!

Energized, and now super anxious to get home, the six of us boarded a train that took us straight to the Mickey Mouse Station. Disembarking, I surveyed the array of cars, some in clusters, others sparsely dotting the park landscape. And since there was no car finder service, my only help was trying to remember where I parked the car.

I was so utterly baffled that I looked around and wondered whether the car too was lost. And since there was no Lost and Found, I decided to sit tight and wait to see the last car in the lot.

By 3:30 a.m., the lot was emptying quickly, but still, no sight of my car. No doubt its grey body color blended with the overhanging morning clouds, like a grey battleship camouflaged against the hazy horizon. So, I waited and waited…Looked, and looked, and looked…And prayed, and prayed, and prayed, not restricting myself to five, eight, or a dozen mental chant sessions. Perhaps, the Divine was the light in the rising sun!

Mentally, I did a quick performance of my *Surya Namaskar*[51] . Then Bingo! The car appeared as if from nowhere—just a few feet away—before my very eyes, staring at me in full view. *Mirabile dictu*: Marvelous to behold!

As the poet Alfred Lord Tennyson wrote, *More things are wrought by prayers than the world dreams of.*

---

[51] Sun Salutation yoga pose

47 SAVED BY A COMMA by Kennard Ramphal

We were sitting in the office of the English department in Bowside High School when Bob Singer, his face contorted with frustration, came in the office. I always felt inadequate in Bob's company, and on that particular day, I felt even more self-conscious. My blue jeans, old brown sweater and sneakers made a sharp contrast to his striped suit and shoes polished to a military shine.

"I've got to teach these students how to use the comma," Bob told us. "Look at these two essays. Elaine put a comma after every phrase, and Mike used only three commas in his entire essay."

Another teacher, Sam Bahadur, tall and lanky with shoulder-length hair, who had immigrated from Guyana like I did some years earlier, was immediately interested. "The comma is extremely important," Sam emphasized. "Last summer, I went to New York and a comma, really the absence of one, saved my brother in Guyana from getting a *bad name*[52]."

All the teachers leaned back in their chairs and smiled. We recognized that Sam had a story to tell about almost everything, and although we were busy, and classes were due to start in fifteen minutes, we took a break from our evaluation of students' assignments to listen to Sam's story, because his accounts were always very detailed and interesting.

Sam leaned back in his chair, clasped his fingers, and put his hand around his stomach, before recounting his experiences...

Last summer, my wife and I made our first trip to New York since we immigrated to Toronto, I hadn't seen my sister and brother, both younger than I, since they immigrated to New York three years ago. My sister, Kamla, and her family live in Queens, while my

---

[52] Slander spread by someone.

brother, Balram, and his family reside in the Bronx.

I had known Kamla's husband, Ramraj, before he started courting my sister, because he was working in the office at Diamond Estate, and I was teaching in the primary school in Grove. Of course, we became closer when he frequently visited our home in Windsor Forest. Whenever he visited, my elder brother, Abel, and I entertained him the only way we knew. We took him to the local rum shops, in spite of the fact that Ramraj was not much of a drinker. Whenever we went to one of the watering holes in the village, he would mix a few drops of rum with almost a quarter bottle of Pepsi, and we would tease him that he was drinking most of our chasers. I was therefore surprised to learn that he was drinking quite heavily in the United States.

Two years after he and my sister were married, Ramraj left Guyana to study accounting in the U.S., and decided to stay in that country. Kamla joined him later, and their two daughters and son were born the U.S. Ramraj was proud to tell anybody who would listen that his children were American citizens by BIRTH, making sure that he emphasized the last word. Balram joined them the following year, and got married to Beatrice, a nurse, who sponsored him as a resident. They settled in the Bronx, where they raised three fine sons.

Sam took a sip from the red mug on his desk, which was half-filled with coffee, and continued his story....

We knew that Ramraj was an emotional person, and I deduced from his many phone calls from New York to Toronto, often late at night, that he was becoming even more so, especially after he had had a few drinks.

My wife and I traveled on a flight arranged by *The Last-Minute Club,* and the airline with which we flew had declared bankruptcy between the time it flew us to JFK Airport, and the time we were scheduled to return to Toronto, but that's another story.

**

Kamla, dressed immaculately in a pink sari and colorful sandals, met us at JFK Airport at about two in the afternoon, and drove us in her blue Toyota Corolla to her home in Queens. As we drove along the highway, I looked forward to eating her chapatis and a variety of curried vegetables because as a vegetarian, Kamla cooked and ate no meat.

When we arrived at her home, I was surprised to see Ramraj standing in front of his doorway with a roll of carpet under his arm. *Why the carpet under his arm on a hot, summer day?* I asked myself. Ramraj was below average height, and he seemed to have shrunk a few inches since I last saw him in Guyana. He had a full head of white hair, and his face was covered with a few days' worth of stubble. Kamla indicated to me that my family and I should precede her through the wrought iron gate leading to her house, and as soon as we entered the gate, Ramraj rolled out the carpet with a flair. I noticed that the carpet was bright red, and realized that my brother-in-law was literally giving us the red-carpet treatment.

"Welcome to my home in the UNITED STATES," Ramraj said, emphasizing the last two words. Then he started crying as I walked up to him and hugged him. He refused to let go of me until Kamla intervened.

"Sam, everybody gone in the house, and Balram and Beatrice waiting for you. You got to come in now. Ramraj gets emotional and starts to cry because of any little thing."

I disengaged myself, and followed my sister into the house, with Ramraj trailing. He had left the red carpet on the concrete strip as a reminder of his colorful welcome to us. My brother, Balram, and his wife, Beatrice, were standing inside the house, impatiently waiting for us to join them. Apparently, Ramraj had requested them to leave him alone so that he could welcome us in his dramatic way.

After greeting my brother and his wife, the first thing that caught my eye was the welcome sight of a half-gallon bottle of Chivas Regal sitting majestically on the coffee table, surrounded by crystal glasses. Ramraj had previously justified his excessive drinking to me by arguing that he always drank cheap whisky, but had obviously made an exception for my visit.

Ramraj had stopped crying by this time, and proudly instructed me: *Sam, you take the maiden.*

I happily obliged, and Balram, Ramraj, and I settled down and enjoyed the fine scotch. We finished almost half of the bottle, and stubbornly ignored Kamla's consistent exhortations to *come and eat.*

After the third time Kamla asked us to eat something Ramraj suggested, "Why don't you bring us something to act as cutters? We will snack as we drink."

Then he turned to me and Balram, and offered his expert advice. "When you eat too much, you become bloated, and you can't drink any more. When you drink and eat a little bit of cutters now and again, you can drink the whole day."

Both Balram and I nodded as we poured another drink. A few minutes later, Kamla brought a plate of pakoras, potato balls, and sauce which she placed on the coffee table. We reveled in each other's company as we snacked, drank, shared jokes, and reminisced about the good times we had in Windsor Forest. The more I drank, the more I missed Abel, older than I by eighteen months, and regretted thar he was unable to get visas for himself and family to come to either Canada or the U.S.

I couldn't help telling Ramraj and Balram, "I wish Abel were here."

Ramraj put his glass on the coffee table, looked at me and started crying. I surmised that he was crying because he also missed Abel, and I attempted to console him.

"Ramraj, Abel, you and I had some good times, in Guyana. I know that you miss him, but we'll meet up again some time."

"You, Abel and me were so close." Ramraj held up his right hand, and placed his index finger on top of his middle finger. "I never imagined that Abel wanted me to die."

"Abel would never want that," I quickly countered. "I know that he likes and respects you very much. Except when you drank all of our chasers," I quipped.

"I have it in writing," Ramraj said between sobs. "I kept the letter, because I know that nobody will believe me. I gon go and get it for you," he continued as he walked up the stairs, leaving me and Balram looking at each other with disbelief.

Ramraj went up the stairs, returned with a letter, and pointed to the underlined part. Abel had written: *Ramraj, that bastard didn't die yet. If he doesn't die soon, I may die of vexation.*

"You see? What more proof do you want?' he said.

My mind was numbed by numerous drinks of Chivas Regal, and I still tell myself that I am a good reader, and had I been completely sober, I would have picked up the meaning of the letter immediately. I held the letter, and thought of my brother. *Abel likes our brother-in-law. Why would he write this?*

Another excuse I still make to myself for not reading the letter accurately, was that Ramraj had set me up as a reader to anticipate that Abel wanted him dead, and I read the letter with that mind-set.

Then, I showed the letter to Balram, who looked at the underlined parts, threw a school-master's look at me, then turned to Ramraj, "You ever heard of the noun in apposition?"

"How you gon explain what Abel wrote?"

Balram leaned towards Ramraj, "Did you ask Abel why Burnham wasn't dead yet?"

"Everybody wants Burnham dead," Ramraj responded. "Since he became president of Guyana, he thieving money and ruining the country. And he ban everything. You can't get flour to make roti. No wonder everybody leaving the country."

"Well, Abel responded to your query—*Ramraj, that bastard didn't die yet. If he doesn't die soon, I may die of vexation.* He didn't want to name Burnham because had somebody opened the letter, he could have been in trouble. But he did NOT put a comma after *bastard*, so that means that he is referring to somebody else. Had he written *Ramraj,* comma, *that bastard,* comma, *didn't die yet,* then he would have meant you. The extra comma meant that the term *that bastard* would be a noun in apposition, and would have referred to you."

I could almost hear Ramraj's brain churning as he took the

letter from Balram and began to study it. I still pride myself that I picked up on Balram's explanation immediately, and I decided that I would not be outdone by him.

"The comma after *Ramraj* means that he is addressing you," I said looking at Balram who was nodding. "*That bastard,* is referring to Burnham."

Ramraj, his face contorted with concentration, looked at the letter for quite a few minutes, and then his entire body shook so much as he sobbed that I had to pry his glass from his hand and put it on the coffee table to prevent his drink from spilling.

"I blamed Abel all these years for nothing," Ramraj said, through his tears.

I looked at him crying hysterically, then glanced at Balram who looked as proud as a peacock that he was able to resolve the miscommunication,

I picked up my glass. "Saved by a comma," I mumbled in my Chivas.

**

Sam Bahadur smiled as he completed his story, and we all sighed with relief that the story ended well.

"Bob, go and teach your students how important it is to use the comma correctly," Sam advised.

Just then the buzzer sounded, indicating that it was time for classes to start, but before he left the staffroom, Bob turned to Sam. "Sam, can I use your story to demonstrate to my students the importance of punctuation?"

Sam nodded, and we all gathered our folders and hurried to our classes, while contemplating the importance of a single comma.

48 DO YOU KNOW THE WAY TO SPRUCE GROVE by Roop Misir

Spruce Grove is a city 11 km west of Edmonton, Alberta, Canada. It is adjacent to the Town of Stony Plain and is surrounded by Parkland County. The year was 1979. Our baby son Anil was barely two years old, accompanying my wife, Ramdai, and myself in the car for the ride to Spruce Grove.

In November, my Professor Wilhelm Bauer, had invited us to visit his home in Spruce Grove for a social evening. We lived in the Hermitage district, Edmonton North East, a distance of about 40 km. away. Normally this trip would be a half-hour drive, but we knew that it would take us longer because of the snow-covered roads. When we left home at 6 p.m., light snow was falling, so, I made sure I was equipped with a full tank of gas, flashlights, and other travel essentials, including jumper cables.

Those were the days before GPS and cell phones. But I did have Dr. Bauer's address and a hand-drawn road map from the Yellowhead Trail W, and secondary roads. Looking back, I would think twice before venturing on such a trip again.

Snow continued to fall, accumulating in certain areas. The roads were getting slippery. At times, the car would sway and fishtail. I was debating whether we should stop and wait by the roadside until the snow stopped, or continue driving to Dr. Bauer's residence, now only about four or five km. away. I continued to drive.

Anil was fast asleep in the baby car seat, so I told Ramdai to make sure that he was comfortable. Then I started humming the tune of the song, *Do you know the way to San Jose?* substituting Spruce Grove for San Jose.

Perhaps I got too absorbed in singing. And before I realized what was happening, the car started sliding slowly, sideways into the ditch adjacent to the edge of the road!

From prairie life experience, I know that when light fluffy snow accumulates on the road, the place seemingly sounds eerily silent. On the highway, some cars whizzed by, and the few that did slow down kept driving. After standing and trying to flag down a vehicle for help for nearly an hour, a farmer with a hoist and some jumper cables stopped.

"Thank you for stopping. I am so grateful," I said.

The kind farmer responded, "Yes, I helped quite a few drivers stranded on the road. I am so tired that I was wondering whether I should stop or be heading home. Then I saw the baby in mommy's arms. I didn't have the heart to pass without pulling your car out and helping get you back on the road again!"

I was happy to hear these wonderful words of concern and determination to help! "My name is Roop," I mentioned. "And you are…?"

"John. They call me Farmer John."

"To me, you are an angel. A good Samaritan! These days a person like you is so very hard to find!" Then I inquired "How much do I owe you?"

"Nothing, absolutely nothing," he retorted.

Then Farmer John offered me winter tips on how to start the car.

Instinctively, he asked me: "Do you know the way to Spruce Grove?"

"Yes sir," I answered.

"God bless! Au revoir!"

Then we headed straight for Dr. Bauer's residence. He and his family were so happy to see us, especially our little infant who was safe and wide awake!

They say acts of God—or things, happen, in strange and mysterious ways.

As I continue my life's journey, I've seen and experienced similar incidents.

EPILOGUE

The baby is now grown up, and married with a child of his own. By profession, he is a medical doctor. His career is devoted to helping to heal the sick and to promote healthy living.

49 A WEDDING INVITATION by Roop Misir

We lived in Saskatoon during the 1980's. At this time, I worked in animal science research at the University of Saskatchewan, Saskatoon. My wife Ramdai worked with the Public Works Department, Government of Canada.

Our three small children kept us busy. On weekends and holidays, we would relax at home, or interact with work colleagues and friends, meeting at shopping malls and other public spaces. Among these were only one Guyanese family, and a few Caribbean people. However, other acquaintances were folks like us PIOs[53], mainly expatriate Indians teaching, or affiliated with the University of Saskatchewan.

Later when Pa and Ma came to live with us, we got some help by way of babysitting and childcare. A former Hindu priest in Guyana, at times Pa would officiate at private poojas, and rarely at weddings.

One day my family received an invitation to a Hindu wedding to be held in Saskatoon, and Pa was named as the officiating priest. Since Pa would need a ride to and from the wedding hall, our entire three-generational family of seven was invited.

Certainly, I was happy to accept the invitation. It would help in cementing bonds with our growing circle of friends within the Saskatoon Indian community. However, there was one request: *No boxed gifts!*

I'd never seen this stipulation before. Gifts were reasonably priced at local department stores like Macleods, Sears, and Saan. Alternatively, cash was king, so money was perhaps more than welcome.

Some folks share the view that gift-giving should be a voluntary

---

[53] People of Indian Origin

gesture, not a requirement—or so I thought. Why? Because it was the wedding couple and household who chose to invite guests. Besides, they would have to budget and pay for their special event before the wedding day. And so, to entice invitees to grace the occasion with their esteemed presence, they gladly issued guests with the invitation. In our case, all seven of us!

As a result, we took no boxed gifts, and no monetary gift—as is now customary. In retrospect, I was out of tune and misinterpreted the info on this particular invitation card. In these changing times, wedding costs in Canada are super-expensive. A once-in-a-lifetime affair!? So, it's the expectation that invitees open their wallets and chip in for the big fat Hindu wedding day. This is in striking contrast to places like rural Guyana and parts of Trinidad & Tobago where anyone can attend and enjoy a free-for-all buffet meal and even drinks, whether they were invited or not.

When a wedding invitation is received, the invitees reserve the right to graciously decline. No explanation is needed. Then others next in line could move up the invitation chain, and pay for the privilege to be guests!

As for this particular invitation, my entire family attended. The reception was lavishly decorated and catered. Favorite drinks flowed freely. The catered meal was sumptuous, topped off with the choicest Indian desserts. We had such a wonderful time!

When it came to dancing, I usually would shy away. But not this time! For the first time, dancing at an invited event was not taboo for me! Thanks to the alcohol catalyst, I was among the first to hit the floor that night.

Our best wishes to the bride and groom and the parents who threw such a lavish celebration for the newlyweds. There and then, it occurred to me: At times, the best things in life are free.

Was I being El Cheapo? Or just riding the wave? However, I didn't feel too bad. I did not crash the party, At least, I was invited.

50 MY APPRENTICESHIP by Kennard Ramphal

Our world is full of unrecognized and unsung heroes. Even though the obituary of Dr. John McInnes was headlined, *The Man Who Taught Young Canada to Read*, and it focused on Dr. McInnes' professional achievements, I feel that Dr. McInnes was not sufficiently acknowledged as a kind, compassionate, and basically a decent human being. I hope that a description of my apprenticeship with him will help readers see him in that light, as well as a consummate professional.

In 1975, I was a recent immigrant to Canada, and I enrolled in a B.A. Honors course at York University where I met Beverley Vilyakainen, who was taking the same course in Canadian Literature as I was. I shared that I was a teacher in Guyana, and that the Ontario Ministry of Education had issued me with a *Letter of Standing*, which entitled me to teach in Ontario. However, I found it difficult to get a job, even as a supply teacher, because I had no contacts.

"An honors degree in English will definitely help you in your job quest," she advised me. "But if you're looking for contacts in the field of education, the best institution in which to be studying is the Ontario Institute for Studies in Education. We call it OISE for short. It is full of teachers, administrators, and supervisory officers studying for their Master's and Ph.D. degrees. When are you graduating?"

"If I continue with my Honors degree, I will graduate in two years, but I can graduate with an ordinary BA this June."

"Why don't I bring you an application for admission to OISE, and you can submit it? If you are accepted, you can graduate with a BA, and then continue your studies at OISE. Believe me, if you are looking for a teaching job, your time will be better spent in an institution where you can pursue your Master's Degree, and network with a community of educators."

I accepted Beverley's advice and submitted the application to OISE which accepted me into the M.Ed. program, with a focus on curriculum. There, it was my good fortune to meet Dr. John McInnes, who was teaching several courses in reading instruction.

Dr. McInnes, who insisted on being called "John," was a kind man with sparse hair on his head, and a welcoming smile. He valued each of his students, although his classes were packed because he was so popular. John taught his classes in the same manner he advised teachers to teach their students, and respected the participation of all his students, regardless of whether they matched his philosophy or not. In addition, he had the knack of making each student feel special.

I remember one occasion when I contributed to a discussion in his class about students liking the sounds of words, regardless of their meaning. During coffee break, I was sitting alone at a table.

John left his group, walked over and told me, "I want you to know that I appreciate your contribution in class."

I sat a little straighter as I stammered, "Thank you. I enjoy your class."

It would have taken only a few minutes for John to do this, but those few minutes made the remainder of his summer course so much more enjoyable for me. I took another course with John, during which I expressed my interest in the type of instruction children who speak the Creole dialect received in reading. John was also the chief editor of Nelsons Canada, a publisher of children's books, and was immediately interested. After the class, he asked me to accompany him to his office.

"What are you going to do after your Masters?"

"I am still looking for a teaching job, and I hope to get one soon."

"A teaching job would be nice," he responded. "You know many creole dialect speaking students are in our school system, and many of them are not succeeding. We need to find out why. You expressed an interest in these students earlier. How do you feel about enrolling in the Ph.D. course? You can do your thesis on how these students cope in the reading situation. I earnestly want to produce books to which these students can relate."

"I am awed at how articulate the students in your class are," I responded. "I never went to a high school, and I took a Wolsey Hall correspondence course to achieve my General Certificate in Education at the Ordinary and Advanced levels. These are equivalent to Grades Twelve and Thirteen. All I had to do was read the notes, and regurgitate the information in the exams. I was not required to even know how to pronounce the words, only how to spell them. Even when I went to the University of Guyana, we did not participate a great deal in class. We listened to the lecturers, read profusely, and wrote the necessary papers and exams."

John chuckled. "You may not have spoken a great deal in class, but whenever you spoke, you had something valuable to say." Then he tapped his head, "I know that you were always participating in here. And judging by your papers, you write very well."

"Very often, people have more confidence in me than I have in myself," I admitted. "If you think that I have the ability to complete the Ph.D. program, I will apply to be enrolled in it."

John shepherded me through the Ph.D. program with the same patience, kindness, and understanding he had demonstrated in his classes. Frequently, I told my admired professor, "John, I know that you are well off, and don't need anything from me. But I promise you that many students will benefit from your kindness."

I have focused on the assistance I received from John, but of course he supported several other students. I learned that during the time I was at OISE, there was a Ph.D. student from Thailand who was planning to return home without finishing her degree because she ran out of money. John, who was quite successful financially and lived in Rosedale, gave her enough money to continue her program, and another professor, Dr. Jim Cummins, type-edited her thesis. I imagined her successfully returning to her home country with a Ph.D. degree because of the intervention of two caring professors.

John also demonstrated his respect for people in his everyday life. When he visited my home for a curry and roti dinner, he had a conversation with my mother. John spoke perfect Standard English, and my mother spoke perfect Creole. I was fascinated as I listened, because they understood each other perfectly, and there was absolutely no condescension on John's part.

For my doctoral thesis, I audio-taped, transcribed and analyzed a number of reading sessions involving Creole dialect-speaking students, and outlined strategies, related to reading instruction and reading materials, to increase the chances of success of these students. The oral defense of my thesis went well, and I graduated with a Ph.D., thanks to John, who moved on to help other students.

Unfortunately, Dr. McInnes passed away in March 2008, and the world lost a great man, but his legacy would live on for a long time in the form of the books he edited, and the people he nurtured as educators. These educators will maintain his legacy in assisting learners in our school system.

Eventually I was hired as a teacher in the East York Board of Education, and although I endeavored to emulate John's behavior, I was aware that I frequently failed. Despite my failures, I earnestly hope that I managed to repay some of the debt I owed this remarkable man.

51 CANADIAN LANGUAGE by Roop Misir

Some years ago, I taught ESL—English as a Second Language—in a Scarborough school to a class of Grade 10 students. Most of these newcomers to Canada hailed from South Asia (Afghanistan, India, and Pakistan). Their English communication skills: spoken, good; written, fair.

At Friday General Assemblies, they would join other students in singing the Canadian National Anthem.

Back in the classroom, one lesson focused on learning the lyrics. Many agreed that they liked singing the anthem. As well, they knew what the words meant.

DISCUSSION

One verse in particular caught their attention:

God keep our land glorious and free!
O Canada, we stand on guard for thee.

Irfan was upbeat. He asked me to discuss the meaning of the National Anthem. I responded to the questions asked.

At the end of the lesson, I announced that the movie *Avatar* was showing at local area cinemas. Other teachers were taking their classes to see the matinee at Fairview Mall, North York. Of course, my ESL students were overjoyed. They loved going to the movies, and this widescreen box office hit excited and filled them with great expectations.

Of course, watching movies is a great way to boost their listening skills. It's an opportunity to hear English used naturally—informal English, slang words, and phrases not often found in books or dictionaries.

ADMISSION CHARGE

The theatre admission charge was $6, plus a $2 fee for the bus, making a total of $8 dollars.

The tentative day and date were set, and I advised students that each of them was required to pay me their $8 by the following Monday.

In class the next day, Mariam put up her hand. "Sir, we are newcomers to Canada. Isn't the movie free for us? Or do we have to pay the eight dollars like the other kids? In the National Anthem, we sing the words *Our land glorious and free.*"

Then Sara interjected: "At the reception party for newcomers, we had a big party. It was free for everybody."

Piyush agreed: "At our Mandir[54] weekend services we get buffet lunches. Every time. Always free."

Gurjeet proudly declared: "At every Gurdwara[55], there is always *langar*[56] free of charge! All day all night. So how come we have to pay for the movie plus bus fare?"

I pointed out that events at community organizations may be free, only because members and businesspeople make generous donations. However, if we need to go places and buy items—e.g., cinema tickets and bus fares, we must pay the price for the tickets.

I added: "If you remember, in our former countries —India, Pakistan, Afghanistan, patrons must pay for movie tickets. They are not free. And here in Canada, we must pay to see movies. Everybody has to pay. Even I have to pay for my ticket and bus fare! If you want to go, then you must pay for both the ticket and the bus fare. They're not free!

"In the national anthem, the words…our land glorious and free do not mean freeness, or free things, or to get things without paying money. For the things we need—food, house rent, clothes, cars, we

---

[54] Hindu temple.
[55] Sikh place of worship.
[56] Meals.

must pay for them. We don't get these things free!"

"Rather, the *Land of the free* means the right to choose—to do things that people in some countries are not allowed to do. You are free to choose the books you read, the friends you keep, the religion you like, the food you eat, etc.

"Even when Santa Claus hands out presents, those items are not free! Somebody—our parents, big brother, sister, must pay!"

ABOUT THE AUTHORS

RAM JAGESSAR
(1947-2023)

The late Ram Jagessar was born in Trinidad and came to Canada in 1985. He was a graduate of the UWI's Liberal Arts Program. A teacher, Editor and Journalist, he co-authored several books with known personalities, and wrote *The Man Who Broke The Lottery* (2018).

ROOP MISIR

Roopnaraine Misir was born in Kingston, Leguan Island, Essequibo River. The second of nine children, the family lived at Windsor Forest, WCD, British Guiana. He studied Biology (BSc) and Science Education (Dip Ed) at the University of Guyana (Queen's College campus). Concurrently, he taught school at Windsor Forest (Primary) and Zeeburg (Secondary). In 1973, he came to Canada to pursue higher studies, obtaining degrees in BSA, MSc (Manitoba), and PhD (Alberta). After years of Animal Science Research, he and his family migrated east to live in Toronto, home of relatives, friends, and Guyanese expatriates. Here he taught school at the Collegiate level. Currently retired, he lives with his wife Ramdai. Together they have three grown children and five grandchildren.

KEN RAMPHAL

Ken Ramphal was born in Canal No. 2 Polder in Guyana. He was a teacher before he joined the Guyana Defence Force as an officer cadet, where he rose to the rank of Captain. Ken was the ADC to the acting Governor General, Sir Edward Luckhoo and the President, His Excellency Arthur Chung, before he immigrated to Canada in 1975. He was a teacher, an antiracist consultant in the East York Board of Education, and an education officer in the Ontario Ministry of Education. He is currently retired, and is the author of six books, including one, which he co-wrote with his sister and brother. He has also published a number of articles in educational journals.

ALSO FROM MIDDLEROAD PUBLISHERS

www.middleroadpublishers.ca

Making Literature See The Light Of Day

All books available at amazon worldwide
ebook versions available from all eBook channels

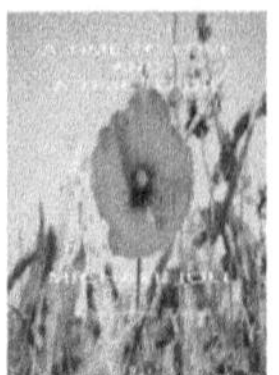

A TIME TO LOVE AN A TIME TO DIE (2020)
By Michael Joll
Finely drawn characters. Visually dramatic, tense and emotionally satisfying, this is one of the finest novels of the Great War. In this poignant story, the writing stands in stark contrast with the unvarnished brutality of trench warfare.

AMAZON

ATTITUDE (2020)
By Dave Moores
Fresh, gritty and laced with dry humour, Attitude is a fast-paced story readers of all ages won't want to put down. It's dead of winter and an outbreak of weird stuff, random acts of vandalism are unsettling the citizens of Southmead.

AMAZON

CIRCE'S DANCE AND OTHER STORIES (2023)
By Heather Laltoo Ferguson
Circe's Dance comprise thought provoking narratives that delve into the complexities of human perception and prejudice. Her stories will

resonate with the reader long after the last page is turned.

Franklin Mohan—author Love Has Two Moons And Other Stories

AMAZON

DANCING MY WAY TO 80 (2019)
By Doris Naraine
Biography published privately and not available for sale.

DOWN INDEPENDENCE BOULEVARD AND OTHER STORIES (2023)
[WINNER 2022 GUYANA PRIZE FOR LITERATURE: FICTION]
by Ken Puddicombe
"A brilliant collection of stories telling the tales of people forced to leave their homes…craving the past, escaping from racial conflicts and dictatorship…"—Judith Kopacsi Gelberger, author of *Heroes Don't Cry*.

AMAZON

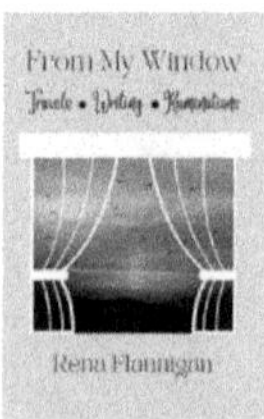

FROM MY WINDOW (2023)

By Rena Flannigan

"A fitting epitaph to a life well lived."—Raymond Holmes, Author: *Witnesses And Other Stories.*

GABRIELLE (2021)
By Michael Joll
Gabrielle transcends time and space, taking the reader on a journey to Poland, France, Holland and Israel as she searches for her identity.

GENERATIONS (2020)

Biography published privately and not available for sale.

I WENT TO THE END OF THE RAINBOW (2020)

by Pramita Chakraborty

A beautifully illustrated, captivating tale

about a young child who can't sleep and embarks on a adventure through the colours of the rainbow.

JUNTA (2014)
By Ken Puddicombe
"A gripping story (of) an imperfect democracy…the tension…builds increasingly from page to page."—Rico Downer, author of *There Once Was a Little England*

LOVE HAS TWO MOONS (2021)
By Franklin Mohan
With humour, insight and sensitivity, Franklin Mohan peels back the subtle layers of prejudice and racism in North American and Caribbean society—Raymond Holmes, author of *Witnesses and other short stories*

MEET ME AT THE FOUR CORNERS (2021)
Anthology
Twenty-six stories, fiction and non-Fiction,

some of them prize winning submissions from the writers of the Brampton Writers' Guild, are featured in this collection.

AMAZON

PEOPLE OF GUYANA (2018)
By Ian McDonald and Peter Jailall
"These beautifully crafted poems are shaped by their generosity of spirit and abundant capacity for empathy and fun…" —Clem Seecharan

AMAZON

PERFECT EXECUTION AND OTHER STORIES (2017)
by Michael Joll
"Michael Joll is a master of surprise endings, but they never seem forced. He always stays true to his characters and their worlds." —Nancy Kay Clark, author and editor, *CommuterLit.com*

AMAZON

PERSONS OF INTEREST (2019)
By Michael Joll
"Exotic and intriguing! Joll brilliantly

captures the reader's interest with vivid imagery and a relentless sleuth." —Phyllis Humby, short story writer, poet and novelist.

AMAZON

POEMS FOR MARY (2020)
By Ian Mc Donald
"The garden which my wife has created, it is as much a work of art as a painting by a master spirit or a piece of perfect music by a composer."—Ian Mc Donald, author, poet.

AMAZON

RACING WITH THE RAIN
(2nd Ed 2023)
By Ken Puddicombe
"Puddicombe's brilliant novel…an historic political conflict in Guyana, during the Cold War and the cold cynicism and tragic irony of a state sacrificed to super-power hegemony." -Frank Birbalsingh, author of *Novels and The Nation: Essays in Canadian*

AMAZON

RUTHLESS RHYTHMS (2022)
By Judith Gelberger
If poetry is a window into the soul of the

author, Judith Gelberger has opened one which illuminates some of the most painful emotions and experiences of human existence... — Raymond Holmes – Author of *Witnesses And Other Short Stories*

AMAZON

SCALING NEW HEIGHTS (2022)
Anthology

Forty-two pieces from the members of Pakaraima Writers Group are featured in this their first collection of poetry and non-fiction travel articles.

AMAZON

TASTE MY WORDS (2022)

By Lisa Freemantle

Freemantle's compositions are imbued with a highly poetic energy instilling in the reader a subtle, penetrating fever of contentment...." — Dr. Franklin Mohan, author *Love Has Two Moons and Other Stories*

AMAZON

THE DARKEST HOURS
By Michael Joll (2023)

The Darkest Hours takes the reader from London slums to the war-torn skies of England and France as characters plot and struggle to survive in a world caught up in the conflict of WWII.

AMAZON

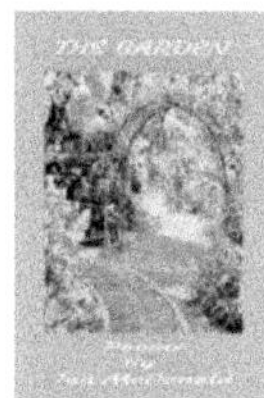

THE GARDEN (2021)
By Ian McDonald

Ian McDonald's poems are full of light and love. His easy style about the beauty of nature connects with his readers.

AMAZON

TOWARDS THE PEBBLED SHORE (2022)
By Peter Jailall

"...thoughtfully conceived, expressed movingly and written with great clarity. I think this may be Peter's best book yet. It lifts the heart."

Ian McDonald, author The Garden and other works

**TROPICAL SCENES
(2023)
By Ken Puddicombe**
"Each poem covers more ground than lengthy chapters." —Cherry Narula, author: *Nona and Daniel, Goldfinch Sunshine Project.*

AMAZON

**UNFATHOMABLE AND OTHER
POEMS (2020)
by Ken Puddicombe**
These poems cover a variety of themes, all connected to a childhood growing up in British Guiana, the rise of nationalism and the pre- and post-independence eras.

AMAZON

**WEALTH THROUGH REAL ESTATE
INVESTING (2021)
By Jay Brijpaul**
Jay Brijpaul has tapped his vast experience and expertise in the Real Estate industry. This book provides comprehensive coverage of What, How, When, Where to invest in real estate.

AMAZON

**WINDWARD LEGS (2021)
By Dave Moores**
A pungent cocktail of choppy romance, corporate larceny and the thrills and spills of sailboat racing, Windward Legs is the rousing and captivating story of a woman's journey to rediscover who she is.

AMAZON